# THE RETURN OF THE EARTH ANGELS

Also by Michelle Gordon:

**Fiction**
The Girl Who Loved Too Much

*Earth Angel Series*
The Earth Angel Training Academy
The Earth Angel Awakening
The Other Side
The Twin Flame Reunion
The Twin Flame Retreat
The Twin Flame Resurrection
The Twin Flame Reality
The Twin Flame Rebellion
The Twin Flame Reignition
The Twin Flame Resolution
The Old Soul's Handbook

*Visionary Collection*
Heaven dot com
The Doorway to PAM
The Elphite
I'm Here

**Children's Fiction**
The Magical Faerie Door
The Magical Mermaid Portal
The Magical Dragon Mirror

**Poetry**
Duelling Poets

**Non-fiction**
Where's My F**king Unicorn?
Finding My F**king Unicorn - The Workbook

# THE RETURN OF THE EARTH ANGELS

MICHELLE GORDON

This book is for all my amazing Earth Angel readers who have waited so patiently for it, I hope you can forgive me for taking so long!

I love you, I appreciate you, and I am sending you so much love.

# AU

## CHAPTER ONE

"You cannot remain, the darkness is too great. It will consume you."

Au felt the love and concern coming from Jr, but it didn't touch her core spark. She knew Jr was right. It was foolish to remain on their dying planet. The darkness had won, and there was no reason to stay.

But this was her home.

"Go without me," Au communicated, moving away from Jr's light. She knew that her friend was radiating as strongly as possible, hoping to touch Au. But Au's light was so dim, it was nothing more than shadow.

"I cannot leave you here. Everyone else has gone already. Started new lives on other planets, or gone to Earth. There is no need to perish here in the cold." Jr shone brighter and moved closer still. "Mg and Tm wouldn't have wanted that for you."

Au felt a cold feeling that she could barely identify, but thought it felt something like rage.

"They left! They don't care what happens to me. If they cared, they would have stayed here. But no! They left, they took their light, and they let the darkness pervade our home! They could have helped us protect our planet, but they chose to try and help the humans instead."

Jr's light dimmed in response to her harsh energy and feelings, and Au felt a glimmer of regret for causing harm to another spark. But the glimmer was snuffed out quickly by her anger.

"Save yourself, Jr, and leave me to the darkness. For I am done."

She moved away from Jr, and retreated to a cavernous room where she had spent much of her days in the darkness since Tm had left her, so very long ago. She hadn't received a message from him since his last one explaining he was still at the Academy, but was in human form so he could no longer communicate with her easily, and had to rely on methods that were far slower. She had no idea if he had received her reply, as it would have taken a while to arrive. Perhaps he had gone to Earth by then.

As a light being, lying was not in their nature, not in their capability. But since the darkness had begun to roll in, lying had become easier. And so, when she had sent the message to say she was in awe of him, and that she thought he was brave, and that she loved him, she hadn't been truthful. Perhaps it was the darkness that now resided in her, but the truth was, she hated him. She would never forgive him for leaving her behind, to be swallowed by the darkness, while he went off to be a hero.

Never.

* * *

Time passed. It could have been days, weeks, centuries,

eons. In truth, time meant very little to Au. She was but a dimming spark of light on a dead planet, with no other sparks to keep her company.

So she really had no idea how long it had been. She didn't know how much time had passed on Earth by the time she got tired of the darkness, and she decided to venture out of the shadows, to see what was left of her home.

After all, what else was there for her to do? Death wasn't really something that happened here. There was always light. At least, there always used to be.

Au drifted about the barren landscape, with memories of light and lushness fading in and out of her energy.

She felt little anger now, just sadness. A deep, complete sadness. Loss, she figured. Another emotion not known to her before. Loss of the light that used to be abundant.

Until the humans destroyed it.

She felt a flicker within, and her light burned a little brighter for just a moment. It was something beyond anger, or resentment. She didn't yet know what it was, but it made her move a little quicker, and make her way through her deserted world, heading through the darkness for the docks.

Her plans weren't even fully formed until she reached the dock and discovered an empty vessel waiting for her. If she'd had a voice and sound was possible, she would have whooped and hollered and thanked Jr out loud for the gift. The pilot must have known that at some point she might actually abandon her home, and give herself another chance.

She merged her light with the ship, and then came to be inside. Though they had dedicated pilots usually, Au knew that all she needed to do was tap into the ancient knowledge stored within her deepest core to be able to fly the ship, and navigate it to where she needed to go.

As if it knew, the ship fired up and her destination came up on the screen. She felt another strong emotion, perhaps something like glee? And she wondered if Jr would have left her a ship if she'd had any idea what Au's plans were.

She highly doubted it. Jr had a good, kind soul, and Au felt a glimmer of sadness at the thought of hurting a fellow spark. But she shook it off, hoping that Jr had found a new home in the stars.

Then she motioned for the ship to launch, and settled in to enjoy her flight. She would fine tune the details of her plan on her way to the Earth Angel Training Academy in the Fifth Dimension.

Had she not had her eyes closed, she may have noticed that as she took off, the planet she was leaving behind was not entirely dark. That a glow still remained.

*   *   *

The beauty of the stars and planets rushing by the windows of her flying craft were lost on Au as she lost herself in her plotting. The farther away she got from her home, the more she lost her sense of what was good, what was right. She had suffered, her planet had died. And it was the humans' fault. They needed to pay for what they had done to her and the rest of the galaxy.

After much time, Au had a plan partly formed, only partly, because much of it depended on what she found when she reached the Academy. She turned her attention to the windows, and after several more hours - days? - she realised something unusual.

The universe was dark. Far darker than she believed it

should be. Where were all the millions of stars? Many had rushed by early in her journey, but the closer she apparently got to the Academy, the darker it became. Had the humans killed more stars and planets than she had realised? In which case, where would the Starpeople reside? Or were they all on Earth, desperately trying to control the destroyers?

Just when Au thought she must have accidentally navigated her craft into black hole, a shining beacon appeared in front of her, becoming bigger and bigger, until it enveloped her craft completely, and she found herself on the other side of the portal, in the Fifth Dimension. The craft drifted to a stop in the docking station outside of what she was told by her control panel was the Earth Angel Training Academy. She moved outside of her flying craft, then concentrated briefly, instructing the craft to go into camouflage mode. The craft appeared to disappear, but she could just about make out the outline. Then she dimmed her light further, so that she was merely a shadow of her light being self. Part of her plan was the element of surprise, she didn't want anyone to know she was there yet.

Where would the fun be in that?

She looked up at the building in front of her and was amused to find that it appeared the Academy had gone through a transformation. The words shining brightly above the doors read 'Academy of Awakened Humans'.

'How ridiculous,' Au thought. 'There is surely no such thing, how can there be?'

Au moved to the entrance of the Academy, a curiosity washing over her. She wondered what Tm had felt when he had arrived there. Was he happy? Excited to become a human?

She couldn't quite imagine being excited about

becoming a destroyer. Even if it was with the intentions of stopping the other destroyers. She merged through the closed front door into the foyer, and was struck by how light the interior was. The floors, walls and ceiling shone and glimmered from within, as though they were alive.

It reminded Au of her own planet, when there had been light. She felt her anger rise up again, and wondered if this was how they had tricked beings into becoming human. With this false light, with the promise of making a difference by bringing their light to Earth.

She moved quickly down the gleaming hallways, towards a large set of doors. She passed through the doors, and found herself in a large, cavernous room, with hundreds of seats in it, and a platform at the front. She went to the platform and looked back at the seats in front of it, and wondered if Tm had sat there once, looking up trustingly at the liars before him, promising miracles they could not deliver.

Her anger simmered further, and she moved out of the cavernous room down the hallways, wondering now why the Academy was so quiet. Where was everyone? Had it closed? Had they given up trying to get the humans to change? Was the universe now just left to its demise, after they had done too much damage?

She moved a little faster now, still no more than a shadow in the gleaming, empty Academy. She saw a sign that bore familiar symbols, and she moved through the door to find herself in a miniature version of the galaxy, complete with meteorites tumbling around lazily, and gravity feeling non-existent.

She thought again of Tm. Had he visited this place? Had he thought of her? Had he regretted leaving at all? Did he miss home?

Afraid that her anger would make her spark burn too brightly and give away her presence, she moved back into the main building. She searched the hallways until she found a corridor that led to the main offices of the Head of the Academy, and the ones who kept operations running smoothly. She avoided the office for the head, which bore the name 'Prof. Brown Corduroy' and slowly merged through the door that said 'Marketing & Operations'.

'Jackpot,' she thought as she spotted the screens and technology that could only have been created by her kin. Yet again, there was no one around, so she wasted no time in heading for the control panel, to see what she could find.

# CHAPTER TWO

Several hours later, Au felt something akin to exhaustion. She wondered if simply being in the Fifth Dimension was giving her the sensations of being human, even without inhabiting a human body.

She had read and watched thousands of digital logs, kept faithfully by someone of her kind, she was sure, and she was aghast.

It was worse than she had feared.

Before she could begin to process and understand the true picture, the full scope of tragedy that was the human race, the room glowed brighter, and she heard voices.

She moved away from the control panel quickly, and moved into a corner of the room where she hoped to remain undetected.

"Good morning, Bk," a small pink flying creature sang out as they entered the room. "Oh," she said, frowning and spinning around in circles. "Could have sworn there was a Zubenelgenubian in here. Weird!" She flew to the dashboard in front of the screens and began waking things up from their digital slumber. When she reached the control panel where Au had been, she stopped suddenly. "What is all this doing out?" She scrolled through the logs that Au had been consuming. "Is Bk on another project without telling me? Sneaky!"

Au dimmed her light even more, hoping that the creature would not sense she was there.

Moments later, the door disappeared again, and a human entered, though Au knew that this was no human, but an old friend. Bk. She remembered now. He had been one of the very first to leave their planet, what felt like many lifetimes ago. It took all her willpower not to glow brightly, to greet him, to communicate with another of her kind. It had been so very long.

"Bk! What have you been up to?"

Bk frowned and looked up from the small device he was checking in his hand. "What do you mean, Dahlia?" he asked the small pink winged creature.

The creature waved her tiny hand at the control panel. "The logs are all open. And I could have sworn you were in here when I arrived."

Bk went over the screen and looked at the logs. "It wasn't me, I promise. But it's weird." He held out the device to the creature. "I have a notification of a craft arrival at the docking station, but I just checked it and there's nothing there."

Au started to move towards the door. If they worked out she was there, she would be trapped. How would she explain sneaking into the Academy? How would she get her revenge on the humans if they knew she was there?

"Maybe you should tell Corduroy?" Dahlia suggested. "Unannounced visitors are rare, there could be a problem?"

"I'll go and speak to him now. Check to see if anything

is missing from the logs, or if anything has changed, and make a note, okay?"

Dahlia nodded and Bk headed for the door, which disappeared to allow him through. Au waited a few moments, then she began moving towards the door. As she slowly brushed past the wall, a glimmer caught her attention. She saw the edges of an invisible doorway, and while the pink creature was occupied, she merged backwards through the secret door.

*　*　*

When Au turned around, she couldn't help the small flicker of light that erupted from her core. She had stumbled upon the mothership. This was where she would find what she needed.

She moved towards the dazzling array of controls buttons, levers, screens and holographics, and suddenly recalled who Bk really was. He had been one of their master technologists. He had created the technology on their planet, and, it seemed, he had created the technology for the Academy too.

Very quickly, Au merged her light with the machine in front of her, and allowed her consciousness to absorb the information she needed.

This machine controlled time. It controlled how it passed and existed at the Academy, and on Earth. The first thing Au did was to take the Academy back in time by six hours. This would ensure that no one would remember suspecting an intruder in their midst. Then she found a seemingly regular day in the life of those at the Academy, and she hit the loop function. She was pretty sure there was some tech in her craft that could run an interference pattern, so that no one could contact anyone at the academy, or indeed visit and ruin her loop.

That took care of anyone at the Academy getting in her way, as they would be kept in a continuous loop of the same day, for eternity. She felt a flicker of both glee and guilt. Guilt that she was subjecting one of her fellow kin to such an existence. Glee that she had begun to execute her plan to make those suffer who had killed her planet.

The next thing she did was to analyse the current situation on Earth. She still couldn't believe that the beings in the Fifth Dimension had been allowed to create what they had. It went against all universal law, surely? And was most likely the reason for the darkness she had witnessed on her journey to the Academy.

In a way, her findings made her plan for revenge both simpler and sweeter. But there was a hollowness to it too. The humans wouldn't suffer nearly as much as she had. But she couldn't stop now.

After watching an analysing the Earth cycles for some time, she decided that the best way to carry out her plan was to create a team. A small army, who would understand why she had to do this.

She set about searching for fellow light beings that were in this Earth system, who could help her on her mission.

She found Tm, and watched his life on Earth. She realised that he was an instrumental player in allowing the humans to experience the Golden Age, and she saw that he had actually fulfilled his mission.

She felt a glimmer of pride at his accomplishments, and her anger for him leaving her to wither faded a little. But where was he now? It was clear that while many humans were trapped in this machine, cycling around in never-ending circles, most Earth Angels were no longer consciously on Earth. They had returned home. So why hadn't Tm come home? The original cycle ended long enough ago that he could have made it back. He must have gone to another planet, or dimension.

Anger glowed white hot in Au's core and she searched the machine for the ability to track beings anywhere in the universe, but it appeared to not have that capability. It looked like she would have to go higher up in the dimension to be able to do that.

Something in the machine came into her awareness then, as she discovered the old Star Program. She saw that the Earth Angels had uploaded their missions and all the knowledge they needed into their star, and then when on Earth, all they needed to do was find the star within, to download the information and remember everything. Though the program was no longer in use, Au realised then that she didn't need her fellow Starpeople to be consciously in their bodies and in contact with her in order to carry out her orders. She could simply direct them like puppets from here through their stars.

If she could have laughed, she would have. They had really made it all too easy. It was a little disappointing just how easy it was, actually.

Shaking off any doubts, Au picked out the key players that she would need to influence, and she got to work.

*   *   *

Her plan now in motion, Au decided to leave the control room, and head back to the weird galaxy she had found when she had arrived. She was feeling greatly fatigued, and needed to plant the interference tech, then rest until she could put the next part of her plan into action. She left the room where Bk and Dahlia were going about their day, feeling a slight twinge at the fact that they had no idea that they had already lived that day before, and that they would live that day over and over again for the rest of their existence.

She emerged into the corridor and immediately shrank back, as a man dressed in brown robes emerged from the room opposite and made his way down the corridor.

It fascinated her that they bothered with human limitations. Walking instead of simply moving to where they needed to be. She wondered why that was, but was too tired to figure it out. She retraced her path back to the main entrance, and after retrieving the tech from her invisible craft, making it invisible and attaching it to the side of the building, she returned to the door that led to the false galaxy. She hadn't seen anyone else on her journey, so she felt it would be safe enough to rest on one of the stars floating about, as her light would merge with it, making her invisible to someone simply passing by.

She found the biggest star, far away from the main path, and came to a rest on top of it. The moment she relaxed, the exhaustion took over her, and for the first time in her existence, Au fell asleep.

# CHAPTER THREE

When Au awoke from her dreamless slumber, she was aware of voices drifting up to her from below her star.

She listened for a few moments, then dismissed the conversation as frivolous and unnecessary. Which proved that her plan was working. The Academy was continuing as normal, with no sense of disturbance from the unwelcome visitor in their midst.

She carefully dimmed her light before she moved away from the star, and then wove in and out of the moving planets and stars, towards the main building. She made her way through the Academy, taking time to merge through various doorways, where it seemed that classes of some sort were in process, with beings that appeared to be simply human. Au couldn't sense any otherworldly-ness to them at all. Perhaps that was part of the Academy's transformation? They now no longer trained beings to be Earth Angels, but merely processed humans who were in the Earth loop? For what possible purpose, Au couldn't fathom.

Satisfied that all was continuing as normal, Au went to the operations room, keen to get back to the main controls to check on the progress of her plan. There should have been a significant shift by now. She also needed to find a way to ensure that the loop on Earth ended. And that the reality that she was currently crafting would be the only, and the last, reality that Earth and everyone upon her would ever experience.

It had gone on long enough. It was time that the age of the humans ended, for the sake of the rest of the universe.

As Au merged into the office, and then moved quickly past Bk and Dahlia to merge into the main control room, it occurred to her that perhaps in seeking revenge for her own means, she may actually be saving the rest of the universe from complete annihilation.

Perhaps she wasn't the villain hell-bent on destruction and death. Perhaps she was the saviour? Her light suddenly glowed brightly and she was relieved that she was hidden out of sight.

A renewed certainty that she was doing the right thing flowed through her, and she turned her attention to the machine.

She had successfully hacked into the Star Program and altered the course of several fellow Zubenelgenubians. Now she needed to check future projections to ensure that this would create the consequences she was seeking. It seemed that in order for the Golden Age to occur (though for some reason it had been renamed the Diamond Age) technology had been hugely scaled back. The Starpeople had not created on Earth the same technology from their planets, they had held back their knowledge. But this was about to change.

It might take a few tries to program their stars to create the most possible pain and suffering for humans, but Au could be patient and work it out. She had waited a long time for this.



Au waited impatiently in the mists. She paced back and forth in the human form that she had managed to conjure, after observing the Old Souls in the Academy manifest whatever they needed.

She now knew the routine of the single day that the Academy was experiencing inside and out, and could move about entirely undetected.

She wondered if she should have given them a loop of a few days instead of just one, as she was beginning to tire of the monotony, but it certainly was useful to know exactly what everyone was doing and when and where.

But today was a big day. Today, things would change. She still wasn't sure exactly how it would play out, but she was excited. And she was enjoying the sensations of her emotions within the human body she had created. Clothed in beautiful golden brocaded robes, her silvery golden hair cascaded down her back, and her fringe framed her luminous golden eyes that had a slightly lighter ring around the pupils. A ring of pure light, showing her true spark.

A sound coming from the mists in front of her made her stop mid-pace, and nervously smooth down her robes and her hair.

She took a deep breath (breathing was something she still had to think about consciously) and projected calm as a figure emerged from the wisps of ethereal energy in front of her.

"Gold?" The figure, a man in his early twenties asked, a confused frown on his face.

"In a manner of speaking, yes, I guess," Au replied, a smile on her face.

"Female, huh? You know, many on Earth believe you to be female. It makes sense, I suppose, after all, you can take on any form you wish, right?"

Au nodded, but her mind was whirring.

Tm did not recognise her. He thought her to be that ancient fool who thought he had authority in this dimension. Yet that fool had been tricked into leaving his post to enter the Angelic Realm, where she had planted a device that would cut him and the Angelic Realm off from any contact with humans on Earth again. They clearly couldn't be trusted to do their jobs properly, so it was up to her to do it for them.

"Gold? Gold?"

Au blinked and turned her attention outward to Tm, who was snapping his fingers in front of her face.

"There you are, where did you go? To another planet?" Tm joked.

Au smiled slightly, if only he knew. But perhaps she should keep him in the dark. If he thought he was doing Gold's bidding, he might listen. After all, he didn't listen to her and stay on their home planet, all those many eons ago.

"You know, I must admit to being a bit confused. I mean, I'm pretty sure I'm not meant to be here right now, unless it will help my writing?"

Au tilted her head to the side. "Your writing? You are here now, you will have no need to write."

Tm frowned. "What? Wait, aren't you going to ask me the ultimate question? That's how it works, right? Humans die, then come here, meet Gold, then they decide if they stay or not. It's a choice. Right?"

Au shook her head. "There have been some changes. No more choices. Humans don't make good ones. You shall stay here now, I need help with something."

Tm held up his hands and took a step back. "Whoa, wait, are you saying that you've dispensed with free will? That I can't go back? But I have a wife, and a career, and a plan. It was a stupid cold, for goodness sake, I can heal, I can survive it."

Au shook her head. "It's too late, I have closed the door for your return. Now, if you'll follow me, I will fill you in on what I need your assistance with."

Tm looked over his shoulder and the mists parted to show that there was indeed no doorway to walk back through. He looked back at Au. "I don't understand." His voice cracked, and Au felt a pang of guilt shoot through her stomach. It was interesting how certain emotions lived in different parts of the human body. But not interesting enough to derail her focus from the matter at hand.

She sighed. "You will, I promise. But you need to come with me now."

Tears rolling silently down his cheeks, Tm nodded, and followed her through the mists, towards the Academy.

*   *   *


Tm looked at the machine, who Au had now nicknamed Nano, confusion plainly on his face.

"What is this? And why have we had to sneak in to see it? Gold, what is going on?"

Au sat down on a swivel chair in front of Nano and gestured for him to do the same. It was still weird, having to adjust to the needs of her human form. She was in awe of how at ease Tm was in his.

"Tm, you have been living a lie. This," she waved her hand at the glorious machine before them, as it whirred contentedly, "is Nano. It is the machine that is controlling Earth and everyone upon her. The life you just left? Wasn't real. It was merely a simulation of a life you once lived, many eons ago. You have been stuck in a loop since that life ended, and this machine is what is controlling that loop."

Au figured that even if she couldn't tell Tm who she really was, she could still be truthful about the current situation, and how she needed his help.

Tm's confusion had turned to horror, and he shook his head. "That's ridiculous. Of course my life was real, I was just there, living it."

"I know that it felt real, as real as anything, but didn't you feel like perhaps, something was off? Something wasn't quite right?"

Tm started to protest, but then paused and frowned. "Well, yeah, I did feel like that. It was a couple of years ago. I suddenly felt like I had woken up from a deep sleep, and I was living a life that I wasn't sure was mine. I could remember things that others around me had no memory of, as if they hadn't happened, and then, and then..."

Au winced slightly. Her reprogramming of the stars hadn't been completely successful if Tm had had memories of his previous life cycles, but it had been an experiment. She may have to make some tweaks.

"And then?" she prompted.

He looked at her. "Things never felt quite right. My wife and I fought a lot, never had time for each other, always seemed to be on our phones, never really present with one another..." He frowned. "I don't think it was meant to be like that. It didn't feel right."

"So you did know. That your reality wasn't real," Au said.

Tm looked at her and nodded slowly. "Well, I guess I did, but I didn't, if you know what I mean. And so, you're saying that it was all just a, a simulation?" He looked up at the machine and let out a tired chuckle. "So *The Matrix* was a true story after all. Is this where I learn Kung Fu?"

Au had no idea what Tm was talking about, but it was clear that he believed her. Which meant it was time to put the next part of her plan into action.

"Yes, I am saying it was a simulation. You were living the same life in a loop, over and over."

"But why, how does that help anyone?"

*Exactly my thoughts,* Au thought to herself. But as Gold, she knew she needed a satisfactory answer.

"The why does not matter," she said. "What is important now is that we end the loop. We had no idea, when we created it, that it would cause the destruction that it has. Which is why I have taken matters into my own hands to end it. I have already begun making changes, which is why things weren't feeling right to you. They were different to your normal loop."

Tm's eyebrows shot up. "What does that mean? You are literally playing God? I mean, first you remove free will and now you are trying to destroy all of the humans by ending the loop?"

Au's anger flared up and she felt her eyes glow brighter in response. She was destroying the humans? Ha! They had destroyed everyone else. It was their turn to suffer. Tm noticed the shift in her energy and he frowned.

"Are you sure you're okay, Gold? There's something

weird going on, you don't seem like yourself."

Au shook herself internally. Though this version of Tm was the humanised version that had been living in the loop, and not the original Tm, the real Tm who remembered his origins, she still needed to be careful and rein in her emotions if she was to get him to do her bidding. "I am most certainly fine," she said. "I am just eager to rectify my mistakes. I should never have set this in motion. It has caused untold damage throughout the galaxy, and it would be most embarrassing if it was traced back here, to this machine."

Tm nodded, appearing to be convinced. "I understand that, I guess. But what harm has this loop caused? Is it really so bad? And is the solution really to end the loop?"

"The loop isn't real," Au said impatiently. "Nothing on Earth is! But in order to end the loop, the human age must come to an end, and that is where I need your help."

"My help? But I'm just an author. I write novels. I'm hardly hero-material."

Au stifled a snort. Running off to be a hero was exactly what he had done when he had left her. But he appeared to have forgotten that. As sad as she was that he no longer knew her, recognised her, she had to remember that he was but a shadow of his former spark.

But this could serve in her favour.

"You are a hero, Tm. That's why I need your assistance. Your planet needs you."

"My planet?" Tm frowned, as though trying to remember a life that hadn't been his. "Wait, I was a Starperson, wasn't I?"

Au nodded patiently. Should she have prompted his memory this way? But she needed him to feel angry, and she knew this would be the way to do that.

Tm gasped as his memory appeared to trickle in. "Zubenelgenubi? Is it in danger?" He suddenly looked aghast. "But that's why I came here, why I became a human on Earth, to save my planet."

"I know, but it is dimming, dying. Without your help to end this loop, it will be gone, lost in darkness, forever." Au's heart thumped hard then, and the grief of her lost home hit her so hard she was afraid she would start crying. When she saw Tm's heartbroken expression, it took every bit of energy she possessed to stop her human form from reacting.

"That's awful, I mean, my kin are there, ones I love..." Tm's head bowed, and Au thought she heard him mutter her real name.

How would he feel if he knew it was too late? That their home was already gone? Their kin already moved on? But Au couldn't let him know that, otherwise he might just give up. She needed to give him a reason to help her. She needed him to feel the anger that had consumed her.

With a sigh, Tm straightened up, and a look of resolve replaced the sadness in his face.

"What do you need me to do?"

*   *   *

"Are you sure we shouldn't be going to the Elders? What about Starlight? This seems like a bigger job than just us, I mean, no offence and all, but, what about Bk and Dahlia? It's kind of weird that we only come in here when they're not here?"

Au was ignoring Tm's questions as she deftly operated Nano to put things into motion on Earth that would shift it to a far more timely ending.

But Tm wouldn't give up. "Gold, please, I know you are worried about being blamed for your mistakes, but are you sure you are not reacting a bit rashly?"

Au chuckled. "This isn't about blame, this is about correcting grievous errors in judgement that should never have occurred."

Tm looked up at the holographic symbols and images swirling in front of them, fear plainly on his face. "But what if we end up making things worse? How do we know this is the correct course of action? That it's for the highest good of all concerned?"

Au couldn't help the snort this time. "How can it not be? The humans on Earth are not real, they are a simulation, they are a manifestation of this machine, which needs to be destroyed. We are not harming souls, we are making things right in the universe. Now, please stop wasting your energy on second guessing me, I must concentrate."

"Okay, shall I leave you be? So I stop distracting you?"

"Fine," Au said impatiently. "But remember," she said, looking at Tm. "You must not be seen. No one at the Academy must know that we are here, they will not understand, and they may try to stop us. Okay?" She turned back to the machine, tapping away at the console. "I won't be much longer, then we will be on our way."

Tm nodded slowly, and as instructed, he took on his true form as a being of light. Au paused in her task to admire his light form for a moment. She really had missed him so.

Then Tm dimmed his light to a shadow, and he disappeared through the secret door.

Au sighed and turned back to Nano. She wished she could take on her light form too, but she didn't in case Tm came back unannounced and recognised her. She couldn't afford for her plan to be ruined now, she had worked too hard on it, and it would soon be time to put phase two into action.

# Velvet

## Chapter Four

"Gold? What the...?"

Velvet's half-asked question trailed off as she stood agog in the doorway, while the Elder's right eye twitched uncontrollably.

"Aren't you going to invite me in?" he asked, a tiny half-smile tugging at his lips. Still speechless, Velvet merely nodded and moved aside to allow him to enter her Seventh Dimension home, where she lived with her Twin Flame, Laguz. She closed the door and waited a moment to gather herself, before following Gold to the main room where Laguz was listening to some old records they had conjured for their evening's entertainment.

"Who was it, Velvet?" Laguz asked, his back to them both as he flicked through the records, which were mostly seventies and eighties classics from Earth. Velvet was still silent, so Gold stepped up.

"Greetings, Laguz, I trust you are well."

Laguz went still, and slowly stood up and turned to face them. "Gold?" he said, his face showing the shock that Velvet felt. "What in the...?"

Gold chuckled. "What indeed. I do apologise for interrupting your evening, but, um, well, the thing is, um, you see, er..." He clasped and unclasped his hands, and shifted his weight from one foot to another. "Er, well, it's um,"

Suddenly terrified, Velvet found her voice and cut him off. "Would you like a drink? I'm sorry, my manners deserted me for a moment, please sit, I'll go and get us all something."

Before Gold could respond, she left the room and headed for the kitchen, where she leaned on the counter, her ethereal heart beating furiously, her breathing shallow.

What was Gold doing here? It had been so long since she saw him last, in the mists, after her last lifetime. But suddenly, memories flooded back, of working together at the Academy, of the times he would show up unannounced, and her whole world being thrown into turmoil. That twitch in his eye... it really did conjure up a lot of fear in her soul. It always meant something big was about to happen, and Velvet didn't like it. She and Laguz had waited an eternity to be together, and she was not about to give that up. Not even for her oldest friend.

Feeling a little stronger, Velvet straightened up, clicked her fingers, then picked up the tray of drinks that had appeared, which fittingly enough, was a round of bloody Marys.

She certainly felt like she was about to go to battle.

*  *  *

It had taken all of her courage and strength to re-join Gold and Laguz in the front room. Velvet had half-considered making a run for it, but she knew there was no way to avoid or escape Gold, he was everywhere, after all.

Velvet placed the tray of drinks on the small round table, and noticed that the two men were sitting in an uncomfortable silence. No small talk. It seemed as though things were worse than Velvet had originally feared.

Despite her disliking for tomato juice, Velvet picked up a glass and knocked back the drink, wishing that it was possible to get blackout drunk. There were times when she missed being a human on Earth. But not very often.

"So, um, well," Gold began awkwardly. "There's no easy way to say this, because, well, quite honestly, it's just not very easy to explain, um, well,"

"Oh, Gold, for goodness' sake, spit it out."

Laguz raised an eyebrow at her tone.

She sighed. "I'm sorry, you being here is triggering all sorts of memories for me right now, and Gold, you're really scaring me. Please, just find a way to say whatever it is you came all the way here to say."

Gold nodded, then took a deep breath. "Earth is in trouble."

Now it was Velvet's turn to raise an eyebrow. "How is that possible? The Earth Angels, the humans, we all experienced the Golden Age, that is, the Diamond Age. Then we all left. The Earth is fallow and resting now. There is no one there to be in danger?"

Gold bit his lip. "Ah, well, yes, there was a change in plans after you ascended and returned here. It was thought that perhaps the humans might like to, well, have another go at it."

Velvet clicked her fingers, and then gulped down the neat vodka that had appeared in a small glass in her other hand. It would have no effect of course, but it did give her the illusion of calming her nerves. "Please, do try to explain what on Earth you mean by that."

"Not everyone was happy to move on, some souls wanted to try their lives again, change things, evolve, improve. And after all, that is what Earth was all about? How could we deny them that? So we created a loop. Now, most of the Earth Angels chose to go home, or to move on to other realms or planets. So it was mostly human souls that decided to consciously remain in the loop. And of course, they were given a choice. Most of them didn't want to experience what lay beyond." He shrugged. "Many are still afraid of what they do not understand."

"I can see why," Velvet muttered. "Because I do not understand, and I am now terrified." She glanced at Laguz, who looked as puzzled as she felt.

"Gold, are you saying that Earth carried on?" Laguz asked. "That humans reside there still? Surely they have run out of resources by now?"

Gold shook his head. "No, I am saying we created a time loop. So that humans could live the last hundred years of Earth's existence over and over. It's a simulation of sorts."

"So how is Earth in any danger then? If the actual planet is resting, and human souls are in a computer game? I fail to see the problem." Velvet was close to manifesting another drink. Her fingers were itching to click.

Gold sighed, and finally reached out for a drink. He took a tentative sip, then a longer one, as though he were delaying his words. "The problem is, we got complacent. We forgot that nothing happens in isolation, that everything is intricately connected and affects everything else."

"You forgot that? The most intrinsic law of the universe,

'we are one'? You forgot?"

"Velvet," Laguz said. He came to sit next to her and put a hand on her knee. The gesture simultaneously soothed and irritated her. But in that moment, she did not want to be soothed. "Gold, please, can you not just summarise what you are trying to say?"

"Okay, you want the short version?"

"Yes, please," Velvet said, making no attempt to hide her exasperation.

"The loop was never meant to be able to affect the reality of Earth, but somehow it has and it is. And now, the Earth is back on the same destructive path it once was."

"The destructive path it..." Velvet frowned. "Complete destruction? Of Earth and other planets in the universe?"

"Yes."

"The destructive path it was on before the great reboot?"

Gold chuckled tiredly. "Yes."

"That's not possible," Velvet said. "We changed everything. I mean, Emerald and Mica, and Starlight, they changed everything. There's no possible way it could have reverted. We lived the Diamond Age. We ascended, and planet Earth was left to renew itself. It's just, it's just not possible."

Laguz squeezed her knee and she became aware that her voice was getting louder and louder.

"Ah, but somehow, that is the case."

"I still don't understand, how?"

"We were hacked. The machine that created the loop was hacked into. And in the same way that I took you back twenty years to before you walked into the sea and drowned yourself, someone found a way to take the whole of Earth back to the early 2000s."

"But that would mean that I am there also? That I, and all the Earth Angels, we are there. Because we were there back then." Velvet looked at Laguz. "But I'm not? I am here, clearly, so how does that work?"

"Your soul can be in many, many places at once, as you know. You are indeed there, but not in a conscious way. In fact, that's exactly what they want. Unconscious Earth Angels are easier to control, to manipulate. Awakened ones cause too much trouble. Also, it is not the original timeline. It is still the rebooted timeline, but it has been tampered with. We assume this tampering is so that it does not reach the Diamond Age."

Velvet sat back in her seat, and tried to process what Gold was saying. It seemed too ridiculous to be true. She frowned. "Wait a minute. Why can't you just get into the machine and change things? Go back to the reality we created? I mean, if none of it is real anyway?"

Gold sighed. "We can't, because that reality is gone."

"Gone? What do you mean, gone?"

"As in, like it never happened. The Diamond Age never happened. They have not just gone back to a loop that we have created. They have taken the Earth back in time to the early stages of that actual reality and wiped out that possible future."

Velvet shook her head, she was finding it difficult to comprehend. "I don't understand, of course it happened, I lived it, it must still exist in time and space, somewhere?"

Gold shook his head. "Only in the memory of the Earth Angels who lived it then moved on. Otherwise, it has gone."

Velvet stood up abruptly. "Um, I need a minute, just, um, I'll be right back."

Without waiting for a response, she left the room and

almost ran through the kitchen to the back door, which had steps that took her straight down to the beach. She hit the sand running, and didn't stop until she reached the water's edge.

*   *   *

The night had set in while Gold had been talking, and the moon shone onto the waves gently lapping the shore.

Normally, these sounds would have soothed her, but not tonight. Tonight, she was fighting a rage that was brewing inside her.

Velvet longed to scream into the sea breeze, but knew that it was pointless. She had once created a storm and brought lightning upon her head, and left her body when she had felt angry and upset. None of that had solved anything, but it didn't mean that she didn't feel like she wanted to do it again.

She sank onto her knees in the sand, instantly soaking her favourite purple jeans. She was oblivious to the wet and she bowed her head and tried to breathe deeply.

She had almost brought her anger under control by focussing on her breath, when a gentle hand touched her shoulder.

"I'm fine, Laguz," Velvet said, not looking up.

"No, you're not."

She felt Laguz sit in the sand next to her and lean against her slightly.

"What's going on?" he said gently.

Velvet sighed. "It's difficult to rein in my human ego at times. The idea that my greatest achievements, my biggest accomplishment of my very long existence has somehow been wiped away, has vanished, as though I didn't sweat and struggle and work so hard to make it happen," Velvet angrily wiped away the tears that fell. "It just, hit me, I guess. What was the point? Of any of it? Of spending so much time away from you? The sacrifices I made, that all Earth Angels made, everything we did, just, gone."

"Those who matter still remember. The Earth Angels remember, that's what Gold said, so it's not completely gone."

Velvet sighed and looked at her love. "I know, it's just difficult to not be human sometimes, and not feel cheated."

"I get it. But at least you got to experience it." He shrugged. "I didn't even get to be a part of it."

Velvet reached out and took his hand in hers. "I still haven't quite forgiven Emerald and Mica for that, you know. For denying us our final human life together."

"Yet we did have a human life together, before the reboot, remember?"

Velvet smiled at him. "We did."

"Yet that only exists in our memories too. So perhaps it's okay that the Diamond Age only exists in the memories of the Earth Angels. Perhaps it doesn't need to be the only reality."

"I hate how incredible you are," Velvet teased. "How do you manage to diffuse my anger so completely?"

"Because I know you," Laguz said softly, squeezing her hand. "And I know that nothing you have ever done was pointless. It all meant something, it all means something."

Velvet shivered as a breeze blew her long dark hair back, and Laguz got to his feet, pulling her up with him.

"Let's go back inside. Gold will be thinking we've run away."

Velvet looked up into Laguz's green eyes. "We could, you know. We could leave this dimension, and make a new life elsewhere. Maybe the Ninth? Or the Eleventh? I've heard great things about them."

Laguz frowned. "Don't you want to hear the old man out? He clearly has more to say, and he must have come here to tell us all this for a reason."

Velvet closed her eyes. "That's what I am afraid of. From the moment I opened the door this evening to find him waiting there, I have felt such terror in my heart."

Laguz pulled her into his arms and held her tightly. "It's going to be okay. And whatever he has to say we can handle it, okay? Together. Because I am never leaving your side again."

"You better not," Velvet muttered into his shoulder.

He chuckled, then released her, taking her hand and leading her back up the beach towards their home.

# CHAPTER FIVE

Gold was still sat in their living room when they got back, but a jazz record was playing softly on the old turntable in the corner of the room. He stood up on their entry and waved awkwardly to the turntable. "I hope you don't mind?"

Velvet smiled at her old friend, and shook her head. "Of course not. I apologise for my behaviour, the human ego, it rears up occasionally still."

"You have been a human for a great deal of your existence, it makes perfect sense."

Velvet and Laguz sat down on the sofa and Gold sat back down in his chair.

"Can I get you any snacks?" Velvet asked, still finding a desperate need to stall the conversation from going to further.

Gold shook his head. "I should be heading off soon, it's just that, well, I feel like I haven't quite got to the heart of the matter."

Velvet sighed. "I had a feeling there must be a reason why you are telling me all of this. And I assume it is not for my programming or hacking skills, because I can assure you, they are completely non-existent."

Gold chuckled. "No, no, I'm not here for your help with the machine."

"So why are you telling me all of this? I mean, surely that is the solution? Find someone who can get into the machine and undo the damage?" She frowned as something occurred to her. "Oh, Gold, I do hope that you are not going to ask me what I think you're going to ask me."

"I'm afraid I am," Gold said. "Because I don't know of any other soul up to the task."

"No, I won't," Velvet said, vehemently shaking her head. "Uh, uh, not happening, no."

Laguz sighed. "You want her to return? To Earth?"

"I see no other way. Earth cannot be left to ruin, we have no way to gauge the ripple effect that might have. It could destroy the galaxy."

"I won't," Velvet said, aware that tears were forming and beginning to fall. She grabbed Laguz's hand and squeezed it. "I have paid my dues, I have done my bit, and I deserve to spend eternity here, with my love. It's not fair of you to ask this of me, Gold, you know it isn't."

Gold nodded. "I know. And I'm afraid that you will also have to ask the same of your old friends. We need as many awakened Earth Angels as possible."

"You want me to ask my dearest friends, who have earned their retirement as much as I have, to go back to Earth, AGAIN, to save the world, AGAIN?"

"Yes, you will need their help."

Velvet shook her head. A memory surfaced then, of a time, so long ago, when her fellow Old Souls stood up, one by one, and pledged their intention to go with her to Earth, to help her awaken the humans and experience the Golden

Age.

She just couldn't believe that it was happening all over again. It was the worst déjà vu in the universe.

"What about me?" Laguz said. "Am I going too?"

Gold shook his head, "You were not on Earth at that time, and I have no way to let you enter as a walk-in, that program was also disabled."

"But," Laguz looked at Velvet, and gripped her hand tightly. "We won't be separated again, Gold. You cannot ask that of us."

Gold sighed. "I may yet need your expertise at the Academy, so you will be able to help Velvet, just from afar."

A sob broke the silence then, and the two men looked at the Old Soul, who had tears streaming down her face.

"Perhaps I should go," Gold said uncomfortably. "Take tonight to consider it, please. I will be back in the morning."

Velvet nodded, but didn't speak. Laguz squeezed her hand then stood up to let Gold out.

Velvet's head was filled with questions, but only one really stood out, screaming at her.

How could she live yet another life on Earth without her Flame?

*   *   *

Velvet lay awake in bed next to Laguz, listening to his breathing. Sleep was not forthcoming, and she did not imagine it would be possible to rest at all. Not that it was necessary in the Seventh Dimension. She and Laguz had created their life to mimic the last human life they remembered having together, and did everything in a very human manner. They ate, drank, slept, read books, listened to music, watched movies. But none of it was necessary. Or even… real. It was all constructed from their intentions and desires. And their need to live their lives in the same manner that they would have in Atlantis, all that time ago, or at the Twin Flame Retreat, in their most recent time together.

Velvet got out of bed quietly, so as not to disturb Laguz, and slipped on her robe and slippers. She left the bedroom and headed down the stairs to the living space below. She ran her hand along the walls as she did so, needing to feel something solid, even if she knew it wasn't really there.

Their house was also a mixture of their house in Atlantis and their retreat in Wales. The same colours, artwork, decor, soft furnishings. It felt like… home.

She went to the front room which overlooked the ocean, and sat on the piano bench. It was here, that she had found Laguz, playing their song. When she had returned to find him, after her longest life on Earth.

She softly played a few notes, and the sound was like a whisper of the past filling the room. She closed her eyes, rested her hands on the keys, and began to play. Softly at first, knowing that it might disturb her Flame from his rest. But soon, she lost herself in the music, and played as though her life depended on it.

When the last note hovered in the air, she felt a hand on her shoulder, heard her name spoken softly over the distant crashing waves.

"You know that we will always find each other, don't you?"

Velvet bowed her head, her hands fell into her lap and she let the tears fall. "I know."

Laguz pulled her upright and enveloped her in his embrace. "Gold needs you. He wouldn't be here if he didn't.

It won't be for long, you'll be back here before you know it, and we will have our eternity together, here, in our home."

"Do you promise?" Velvet whispered into his tangled long blond hair.

"I do," Laguz said. "I will go to the Academy to see what I can do to help, then I will come back here, and I will wait for you."

Velvet nodded, tears still spilling over. She knew Laguz was right. She couldn't turn away the Elder, even though she desperately wanted to run away with Laguz to the furthest dimensions in the universe. She would have to find some reserve of strength from somewhere to carry out this mission.

"Let's go back to bed," Laguz said. "We will find out everything we need to know when Gold returns."

Velvet nodded and allowed Laguz to lead her back upstairs, where she got back under the covers, and pressed her body close to his. She closed her eyes, even though she didn't think she would be able to sleep, knowing that this might be the last night in a long time that she would feel her Flame next to her.

*   *   *

Velvet was surprised to be awoken the next morning by the sound of Laguz in the kitchen. She was glad that she had managed to rest, after all. Though she did miss having dreams. She wondered why she never dreamed in the higher dimensions. Surely it must be possible?

She stretched out, watched the dappled morning sunlight on the wall, and sighed. It was beautiful here. They had created their own paradise. She had felt nothing but love and gratitude for every moment of her time here with Laguz.

But now she had to leave it all behind. She had to leave her home, and fight some being who wanted to destroy Earth.

She frowned. She didn't even know who or what she was fighting. Gold hadn't mentioned who had hacked the system or who was creating the chaos.

That would be her first question for him that morning. She heard Laguz whistling in the kitchen below and smiled. She would have a shower then join him. From all the clattering it sounded as though he was making them his famous breakfast. Even though they could manifest whatever they wished with the click of their fingers, they often still cooked food as they had in their human lives, it brought a great deal of satisfaction, and of course, meant that it tasted so much better too.

After a long, hot shower, Velvet emerged from the steamed up bathroom into the bedroom. She clicked her fingers to dry her hair, (one thing she did not miss was using a hair dryer) and then dressed in her favourite outfit – her purple jeans, and pale lilac knitted jumper that felt like she was wearing a cloud. She put on her shoes, ran a brush through her hair, and then stood at the full-length mirror.

She didn't look like an ancient Angel of Fate about to go into battle with dangerous, unknown forces, hell-bent on destroying the world. She looked like a twenty-something entrepreneur who ran her own vegan café.

Velvet sighed. She could always change her attire later if necessary. For now, she wanted to just feel like herself. Her carefree, happy self.

She looked around the room, taking in the sight of the

messy bed, her bedside table stacked with books she had been hoping to read, Laguz's clothes strewn on the floor, and her own clothes draped over the back of her favourite reading chair.

She could have clicked her fingers and made the room spotlessly clean and tidy, but she didn't. This was how she wanted to remember it. This was what she wanted to come back to.

Before she could change her mind about leaving and dive back under the covers, Velvet took a deep breath and left the room, heading downstairs to her love.

# CHAPTER SIX

"Good morning, Velvet."

Velvet stopped in her tracks in the entrance of the kitchen. She hadn't expected Gold to be there already. But there he was, sat at the breakfast counter. His damask robes seemed incongruous in the modern kitchen. The mug bearing a rude slogan and the stack of pancakes in front of him also looked out of place.

"Good morning, Gold," she replied, heading over to where Laguz stood at the stove. She kissed him on the cheek and then went to the coffee pot to pour herself a cup. "You're back early?"

"My apologies, I know you have never been an early bird, but, well, time is of the essence, and if you were to decline helping me, then I was going to need to consider alternatives as soon as possible."

"There are alternatives?" Velvet asked, hope rising in her chest. Perhaps the fate of the world didn't have to rest on her shoulders this time?

"Um, well, no, but I would need to find some, if you said no."

"Oh," Velvet said, the hope dissipating. She stirred some milk into her coffee and took a sip. She wondered how long she could wait before telling Gold her decision. She wanted to make him sweat a little.

She sat at the breakfast counter opposite the Elder, and Laguz set a plate in front of her. She smiled at him in gratitude, and reached for the maple syrup. She poured a generous amount and started eating.

"So, um, have you had time to consider?" Gold asked, his right eye doing its usual nervous dance.

Velvet swallowed her mouthful of pancakes, and then nodded. "I have, but I have some questions first."

"Ask away," Gold said, looking cautiously optimistic.

"Who is it? Who is the hacker? The one trying to destroy Earth?"

"Ah, well as far as we can ascertain, it is a Starperson of the name Au."

"A Zubenelgenubian? Really? That's surprising. They are light beings, they have no malice. Or at least, they didn't use to. It was the Synapsians that had a more cunning, manipulative energy." She frowned. "And is Au operating alone? Or do they have a team?" Velvet ate another mouthful of pancakes, savouring their fluffy texture and the sweetness of the syrup.

"They came alone, but now they have many Starpeople working with them, on Earth and in the Fifth Dimension."

Velvet swallowed her food and raised an eyebrow. "He's worked fast, then."

"She, I think. Yes, she has wasted no time."

Velvet sighed. "Okay, so if I say yes, if I come to help, I'll just go back to my teens? Become awake in my body, what, in the early two thousands? I wonder if I will still be able to follow the same path? I guess it depends on what changes she has already made."

Gold coughed and shifted uncomfortably in his seat. Laguz looked over from where he stood at the stove and Velvet caught his eyes. She did not think she would like what was about to come out of the Elder's mouth.

"Um, not quite. You see, Au took the world back to the year two thousand, it's true. But, well, she managed to lock those at the Academy into a loop, as well as cut myself and the Angels in the Angelic Realm off from contacting anyone. It, well, it took us quite some time, before we were able to escape."

Velvet's eyes widened. "Wow, well, how much time? What year is it on Earth now?" She shook her head. "I can't believe she imprisoned you all, that's awful."

"It was Corduroy who saved us, he and Bk. And um, well, the year is now 2023."

Velvet's fork fell out of her hand and crashed onto her ceramic plate. Her mouth dropped open, and her heartbeat thundered like the ocean in her ears. "What?" she gasped.

Gold nodded. "Yes, she has had a twenty-three year head start, I'm afraid."

"But surely we can just go back in time?"

Gold shook his head. "No, as I said, the machine we need for that is rigged now. This reality that she has created is the only one that exists."

"Well why don't we find her and get her to unrig it? She is just one Starperson, surely it cannot be that difficult."

Gold sighed. "She is no longer in the Fifth Dimension. She walked onto Earth with another Starperson, who she had helping her. Once they left, the walk-in program was destroyed, stopping anyone from being able to walk in and help, as Pearl and the Angels did, so long ago." Gold set his fork down and sighed again. "I promise you, I have considered every possibility, every solution, and asking you to go back was really the last thing I ever wanted to do. You do deserve to be here, with Laguz. You deserve your retirement, and I hate to be the one to ask you to abandon it. But I really cannot see any other way."

Velvet looked at Laguz, and he nodded. She took a deep breath and looked at Gold. "I understand that, and I will of course come with you. I just needed to know what it was that I was facing. And to make sure that there wasn't an alternative."

Gold smiled in relief. "I knew you wouldn't let me down, you never have, in all these millennia that I have known you."

Velvet sighed. "Of course." She picked up her fork again. "Leave after breakfast?"

Gold picked up his mug and held it up as if to toast her. "Of course."

Laguz sat at the breakfast bar next to Velvet, his leg touching hers under the counter. She looked at him and he began to eat. He reached out to squeeze her knee and she smiled at him.

No matter what happened, she knew that she would be back, and that they would be together again. She just had to hold onto that, and everything would be fine.

As if he were reading her thoughts, Gold broke the silence.

"You'll be home before you know it, I promise."

* * *

"Are you telling me you had this hidden here at the Academy this whole time? Right under my nose?"

Velvet studied the machine before her with a mixture of awe, disgust and irritation. She had insisted on accompanying Laguz and Gold back to the Academy before she visited her friends in other dimensions, so that she could learn everything possible about what she was about to encounter.

"Not quite," Bk said sheepishly. "It was very basic, back when you were head of the Academy. After the reboot, I stayed here rather than return to Earth, and I gave it some modifications, some updates and boosts. I figured we should have some sort of backup mode for the stars, in case something went wrong."

"You had to back up the cloud?" Velvet said with a snort. "Bk, how on Earth did we ever date? You're such a geek."

Bk chuckled, looking pleased that she wasn't too upset with him. "You were just lucky, I guess."

Still shaking her head, Velvet looked at Gold and Laguz. "Well is there a way for you to show me the damage she has done? Like a replay button? I need to know what I am facing here. Also, I will need a recap on my own life, so I don't appear to have amnesia."

Gold nodded and gestured to Bk, who reached out to touch a few of the dials and buttons. He motioned for Velvet to sit on the chair in front of the holographic screen, and a moment later she was enveloped in a hyper-real, high-speed movie of the last twenty-three years on Earth.

When it finished at the present day a few moments later, she felt motion sick. And exhausted. She slumped back in the chair. "Oh, my dear sweet goddess." There were stronger words she wanted to use, but even they didn't convey her utter dismay.

"It's difficult to be certain exactly what Au is responsible for causing, but anything that differs from the reality you lived is likely."

"So, all the biblical stuff then? Wars, plagues, famines, floods, fires." Velvet rubbed her eyes. "I didn't even realise Zubenelgenubians were religious."

"We're not," Bk said softly. Even though he knew she was just joking.

Velvet opened her eyes and frowned at Gold. "What did we do to her? Au? This is revenge, is it not? Some sort of retribution? What did the humans or Earth Angels do to her? There must be something."

Gold shook his head, it was Bk who answered.

"Zubenelgenubi is dead. The planet is devoid of light. Au was the last soul to leave there. It died because they all left to try and save Earth."

Velvet sighed. "Poor soul. We killed her home, so she kills ours? A planet for a star? Are you sure she is not religious?"

"She is angry, very angry," Bk said. "Which is not something we have within us, we are pure light. But a darkness has developed, grown and evolved within her. She was alone there in the dark for a very long time."

Gold added. "She also believes that the loop we created has continued to detrimentally affect the rest of the universe. That it is spreading darkness."

Velvet frowned at him. "Is it?"

"No," Gold said gently. "And if she had reached out to us, we could have explained that. The planets and stars are simply going through their cycles. In time, her own star would regenerate, and there would be light there again.

Just as Earth was regenerating. But it takes a long time. Her actions now are going to ensure that Earth will never regenerate, and will never recover. Which will have a far worse ripple effect on other planets."

"How do you know all this?" Laguz asked. "How do you know what she is thinking, or planning?"

"We were informed, by a Starperson that she recruited to help her. He was suspicious and he left behind a message to help us. Before he was taken back to Earth with her as a walk-in."

"Who was it?" Velvet asked, thinking what a brave soul he must be.

"Tm," Bk answered.

Velvet smiled. She remembered Tm. In the original reality, he was the first trainee to be called to Earth, and in the reboot, he had been instrumental in the shifts, with his books, and his teachings. "Oh, Tim," Velvet said. "I do hope he is okay."

"We hope you will be able to make contact with him when you get there."

Velvet nodded. "I will do my best. Can I now see my own life from 2000 on? I need to know what has changed for me personally."

Velvet didn't see the looks exchanged by Gold and Bk as the Starperson reached out to touch a dial. But by the time the holographic images swirling around her came to a stop, Velvet was shaking her head in disbelief.

"Shit."

*   *   *

"Oh my goddess, Velvet! It's so good to see you!"

Velvet saw a blur of brown corduroy rushing towards her before becoming enveloped in a strong, familiar embrace.

"Corduroy," she laughed. "It's good to see you too."

He squeezed her tightly, holding her perhaps a few moments longer than was strictly appropriate, before letting go and turning to cordially shake Laguz's hand, and nod to Gold.

"So the cavalry have arrived, eh?" he said, moving back to his desk and perching on the edge of it.

Velvet reached out to take Laguz's hand. "Something like that. Laguz is going to stay here at the Academy for a while, to see if he can help with reconfiguring the machine, and I will be going back to Earth. But first, I will be tracking down Earth Angels to accompany me. I have a few in mind who might come."

Corduroy sighed. "I wish I could come with you. I would give that alien hell. Did Gold tell you we were stuck in the same day for over twenty years?"

Velvet's eyes widened. "No, he didn't. The same day, over and over?"

Corduroy nodded. "It took that long for something to break me out of the spell just long enough to find out what was going on. All that time, she was wreaking havoc on Earth, and we had no idea. The human souls that were leaving Earth were on an automatic redirect to the next dimension. It was such an awful realisation." He looked up at Velvet, his expression venomous. "Promise me you will take care of her for me?"

Velvet sighed. "I don't think counteracting retribution with anger is going to help anyone, but I will do my best to get the situation under control."

Gold touched Velvet on the shoulder. "There is no more

time to waste, you must press on.”

Velvet nodded and glanced back at him. “Understood.” She nodded to Corduroy. “You’re doing a great job here, keep going.” Corduroy nodded, looking both pleased with the praise and sad at the same time. She turned to Laguz and kissed him. “I’ll be right back, okay?”

Laguz tried to smile, but it didn’t reach his eyes. “I’ll see you soon.”

Velvet nodded. “I’ll be as quick as I can.” Before she could change her mind, she took a deep breath then clicked her fingers, disappearing into a swirl of purple mist.

# CHAPTER SEVEN

"Still up to your old tricks, even here? Thought you might have retired by now."

Velvet grinned as the Old Soul's head shot up at the sound of her voice. She opened her arms and Magenta jumped up from the small circular table, upsetting the crystal ball which rolled off and hit the floor.

"Um, I'll come back," the soul who had been sitting at the table said. He picked up the ball, set it back on the table and vanished. But Magenta and Velvet were too busy talking over the top of each other to notice.

"What are you doing here?"

"Why did you make it so hard to find you?"

Both women started laughing. Magenta pulled away a little to look at her friend properly. "You look amazing, where have you been all this time?"

Velvet smiled. "With Laguz, of course, in the Seventh. Though perhaps we should have joined you here, in the Ninth. It is quite magical."

Magenta smiled. "It was Tiwaz's idea. Well, after he had forgiven me for leaving him in the previous timeline. It took a little while."

Velvet smiled. "I'm so glad he did. What you did, what you sacrificed, I never did get to tell you how in awe I am of you, really."

Magenta shook her head. "Sometimes I wonder if I did the right thing. I mean, we got to experience the Diamond Age, but at what cost?"

Velvet's hand went to her stomach, and a brief flash of a memory struck her. She had long since forgotten that after what felt like an eternity of trying, she had been pregnant just before the reboot. She sighed. Telling her friend that now wouldn't serve to do anything other than to cause more regret, and she needed her help more than her sorrow.

Magenta sat down at the small table, and Velvet crossed the darkened, incense-filled room to do the same. "So what can I do for you, my old friend? A reading perhaps?"

Velvet smiled. "Well, not exactly."

Seemingly against her will, Magenta's eyes shifted to gaze over Velvet's left shoulder, and before Velvet could say anything, Magenta gasped, and then covered her mouth with her hand. "No," she whispered.

Velvet sighed. It seemed she would not have to explain herself and the favour she needed after all.

Magenta's eyes refocussed on Velvet's, her face now just a picture of horror. "It's all gone? What we created? What we both sacrificed everything for?"

Velvet nodded. "Earth is back on the reboot timeline, but instead of the Diamond Age, it is headed towards certain destruction. And despite it feeling a bit futile, seeing as some things in motion are irreversible, Gold has tasked me with the mission to return to Earth, to at least try to save what I can." She tried to smile at her friend. "And I couldn't imagine anyone else I would rather do that with."

Magenta was silent for a moment. "Earth? Again?" She sighed. "I really thought that I was done, that I could rest easy now, knowing that Earth was resting, that the Earth Angels had succeeded. To go back..." her voice trailed off.

"I know. I thought I was done too. I was so happy with Laguz in the Seventh. We had our home, our life together, finally, after so long without each other. And you and Tiwaz, you have the same. We have both made too many sacrifices, and it breaks my heart to be here again, asking you, again, to give up everything to follow me. But ask I must. For the sake of the universe and all who exist within her."

Magenta sighed. "I always thought it was the Faeries you had to be careful not to piss off, not the aliens."

Velvet chuckled. "Indeed. This was not something that any of us foresaw. Not even the best of Seers."

Magenta shook her head. "I really do not wish to leave Tiwaz again. We waited so long, we were just starting to relax, to enjoy our existence together."

Velvet reached out to cover her friend's hand with her own. "I completely understand. I have just moments ago left Laguz, and already every molecule of my being is screaming at me to return to the Seventh with him. To wash my hands of all of this, to leave Earth and the humans to their demise, and to live the way I have longed to for so long." She sighed. "But I cannot. Not after working so hard to ensure that this wouldn't happen. As one person, I have no idea what I could possibly do to change the trajectory of the planet. But I realise the entire trajectory is this way because of one single person, well, alien, so it must be possible."

Magenta didn't respond. Velvet's heart ached to put such a request to her dearest friend. But she had chosen to ask Magenta first because she thought she would be the easiest 'yes'. She now dreaded the thought of how the others would react when asked.

"We will be back before our Flames have even had time to miss us," Velvet promised, hoping that it wasn't a lie.

After what felt like an age, Magenta finally nodded. "Of course we will. When do we leave? I must speak with Tiwaz first."

"Meet me at the Academy as soon as you are able. We must leave at the earliest moment, it is already 2023 on Earth."

Magenta stood up and Velvet did the same. She pulled her friend into her arms and whispered, "Thank you," into Magenta's ear.

She pulled back and clicked her fingers to leave, before Magenta could try to change her mind. She hoped that Magenta would be true to her word and would meet her at the Academy.

The fate of the world depended on it.

*   *   *

"Well, well, well," Velvet said when she came to a standstill. "It seems there is such a thing as the Thirteenth Dimension, after all."

Mica was the first to jump up from where he and Emerald sat on the bench by a large lake.

"Velvet!" He engulfed her in a silvery black blur and she laughed, hugging him back. "It's so good to see you!"

"You too, Angel Oracle, you too."

Velvet pulled back, and then reached out to hug Emerald, who was now stood next to her Flame.

"So, you forgive us?" Emerald asked her as they embraced.

Velvet frowned. "Forgive you? Whatever for?"

Emerald sighed. "For our deception. For keeping you from Laguz, from remembering him at all. We thought that you might hold some resentment towards us."

Velvet's eyes widened. "Oh, Angels! Of course not, there is no resentment, I promise. Is that why you thought I have not visited?"

Emerald nodded, her green eyes filled with tears.

Velvet pulled her into another hug, squeezing her harder this time. "Oh, my sweet Angel, I would never bear a grudge against you, or Mica. You did what was needed, what was necessary. The only reason I have not come to find you is that I was wrapped up in my own little bubble with Laguz, in the Seventh, and we have been blissfully unaware of anything outside of that. I am so sorry that you have thought you needed to be forgiven!"

Emerald squeezed her back. "Thank you. I'm so pleased you have been happy these last few millennia." She pulled away from her friend, a frown on her angelic face. "But what brings you here, now? What broke your bubble?"

Velvet sighed. "Perhaps we should have a seat," she said, moving towards the golden bench by the lake, which quickly extended itself to easily fit the three of them.

"You have not come to us with good tidings," Mica said, his expression grave.

Velvet shook her head. She had no idea where to begin. She realised now that Magenta really had been the easiest to ask for help, because she hadn't even needed to explain why.

"Earth is in peril, and I need your help to save it," she said, deciding to dive in at the deep end.

Mica and Emerald exchanged looks. "But that's impossible," Mica said. "The biggest threat to Earth was humans, and they have moved on?"

Velvet shook her head. "That was what we all thought, but it seems that Gold and a few others felt the humans should be able to experience their lives several more times, maybe improve themselves? So they created a time loop."

"Ohhh, why do I not like the sound of this?" Emerald said, shaking her head.

"I'm afraid it gets worse," Velvet said.

*   *   *

Feeling weary and in need of a boost, Velvet was glad to find herself at the edge of the water, when she clicked her fingers and intended to find Beryl. She knew that the Angel would have found a stunning place to retire to, and she wasn't wrong.

She walked up the beach, away from the water's edge, allowing the salty air to revive her. She headed towards the blue house right above the dunes.

By the time she arrived at the back door, she was feeling refreshed, and ready for yet another challenging conversation. So far, none of them had gone to plan, and she had doubts as to whether Magenta and the other Earth Angels would indeed meet her at the Academy to go to Earth. In all honesty, she wouldn't blame any of them from abstaining. It was a big ask, especially when there was no guarantee that they would be successful, and no exact date for when they would get home to their Flames again.

She took a deep breath and raised her hand to knock on the door, but it opened before her hand could make contact with the wood.

"Velvet! I thought that purple blur on the beach was you!"

"Beryl," Velvet said, smiling at her friend and opening her arms to hug her. As she held the Angel tight, she realised that though she had lived blissfully in her bubble with Laguz since her last Earthly incarnation, she had indeed missed her friends. And missed having a purpose, a mission. She suddenly realised with a shock that she was somehow enjoying herself.

They released one another and Beryl ushered her into her home, which was light and airy, in hues of blue and green, to mimic the scene beyond the large windows.

Once seated, Beryl smiled at her expectantly. "So, dear friend, what brings you here?"

Velvet smiled back, but was sad to think that her friend would soon lose that very beautiful smile, when she realised that it was not merely a social call.

# CHAPTER EIGHT

It had been a whirlwind of visits to other dimensions, most of which Velvet had never visited before, to ask of her oldest friends a favour that she had no right to ask.

But they had each risen to the occasion and pledged their loyalty to her, to return to Earth with her. Again. Though Emerald and Mica would have to wait to join her, as they had been walk-ins during that last age, and the walk-in program was disabled. She hoped that Bk would be able to fix it quickly so that they could join Velvet and the rest of the Earth Angels.

"Hey," she said softly to her Flame, who was waiting for her on their bench in the Atlantis Garden.

Laguz looked up at her and smiled. He looked as though he had aged an eternity since she left him only earlier that day.

"Hey," he replied softly, patting the empty space next to him.

She sat down and he wrapped his arm around her, holding her tightly to his side. She rested her head on his shoulder and sighed. She stared at the marble representations of them, quite unchanged since the last time they had parted ways in that very spot.

"Are they coming?" Laguz asked.

Velvet nodded into his shoulder. "Yes. I had half-hoped they wouldn't. That they would refuse, and I would have to tell Gold it was an impossible mission. But it seems they all believe in me too much."

"They love you," Laguz said. "As do I."

Velvet sighed again. Her heart felt heavy. "I don't want to go," she whispered.

Laguz squeezed her tighter. "I know. I don't want you to either. But only because I am selfish, and want you to stay with me." He sighed. "We both know that not going is not an option. You would never sit back and allow the destruction of the universe. It's just not in your nature."

Velvet closed her eyes and a single tear escaped and landed on Laguz's robes. "Because I am the Angel of Fate?" she whispered.

"No," Laguz said, pulling back so that he could look at her face. She opened her eyes, the tears now falling freely. "Because you are you. An Angel, an Old Soul, a Starperson, a human. A divine spark of light. You want all humans to feel loved. To experience the best."

"But it's too late for that now," Velvet said. "Au has destroyed any chance of the Diamond Age being experienced by the humans this time, and Earth is nearly beyond repair. All I will be doing is getting myself a front row ticket to watch the destruction in person."

"It might not be too late, change might still be possible."

"How will the humans ever recover from the havoc she has wreaked? All the pain, the suffering? We know that humans do not thrive in that amount of adversity, they need more hope, more light."

"I guess destroying the light was Au's plan," Laguz mused. "Because she thinks we stole hers."

Velvet rested her head on Laguz's shoulder again and breathed in deeply. She felt a tug at the edge of her mind, and recognised the call.

"They are here," she said softly.

"You had better not keep them waiting," Laguz said.

Velvet stood up, and held her hand out to her Flame. He took her hand and squeezed it, but then let go. Velvet frowned and looked down at her palm and saw that she was holding a worn wooden pendant bearing a familiar rune.

"It will bring you back to me," Laguz whispered. "Again."

Velvet's eyes filled with tears. "You're not coming?"

Laguz shook his head. "You need to focus. Leave me here in our garden, and I will see you at home when you return."

Velvet leaned down to kiss him on the forehead. "I will love you for eternity," she whispered.

"Our love will outlast eternity itself."

With her heart feeling like it was going to shatter into a million pieces, Velvet tucked the pendant into her pocket, and then clicked her fingers.

* * *

Velvet paused outside Corduroy's door for a moment, so that she could clear her tears and compose herself. Her oldest friends in the universe were waiting for her, and they needed her strength, not her fears, her sadness, or her tears. She straightened up and marched forwards, the door only just disappearing in time.

Her broken heart swelled and repaired itself slightly at the sight of the roomful of Earth Angels who had agreed to come back. In fact, there were more than she was expecting.

"Aria?" she gasped.

The green Faerie zoomed towards her, her usually smiling face looking grave. "Oh, Velvet! When I heard what was happening, I couldn't let you all go without me. I also sent word to the dimensions where the other Faeries went after the Diamond Age, so I hope there will be more who will join us. I figured if Tm is involved, I might be able to help."

Velvet smiled at the Faerie. "I am so glad to have you here, the more awakened Earth Angels we have, conscious of the situation, the better."

She turned from the small green Faerie to see that she had the attention of all in the room, so she addressed them all. "Thank you, thank you all for coming, for agreeing yet again, to assist me on this mission." She looked around at the familiar faces, all bearing a degree of fear along with stoicism.

"It's not going to be easy. The level of destruction is extreme, but we must try to find Au, find her accomplices, and put an end to her plans. She must be told that this plan will surely destroy the whole universe, and that it is not the fault of the loop that her planet died."

"Do we know that to be the truth?" a voice from the back of the room asked.

Velvet recognised the Angel's voice. "Hello, dear Amethyst. Yes, we do know that to be the truth. Au may well end the era of humans, but she will likely destroy other planets too. And I'm sure that even as upset as she is, that is not something she really desires."

"But should the loop continue?" Magenta asked. "It does feel to be against what we set out to achieve. If it didn't exist, and the world of humans ended as it should have at the end of the Diamond Age, then we wouldn't be in this position right now."

Velvet nodded at the Seer. "I completely agree. I don't think it should exist either, and I have made my feelings clear to Gold on this."

"I'm surprised that the Angels went along with this loop thingy," Aria said. "Didn't they realise it would be a bad idea?"

"We should have stopped it," Athena said, her voice grave. "But we have always had a soft spot for the humans on Earth, we didn't see the harm in letting them continue."

Velvet nodded. "Well now that we do know the consequences, I hope that Gold and the others will rethink the whole thing and resolve the loop, so that it ends and the humans move onward."

"I shall stay here and see that the loop is ended. It is the least I can do, for my part in the chaos. Besides, I was not there in the Diamond Age, so I could not return unless the walk-in program is revived."

Velvet nodded to the Head of Guardian Angels. "If we cannot find Au and bring her back to undo the damage she has done to the machine, and things on Earth continue to spiral, then I'm afraid the only option may be to destroy the machine, and hope that all the souls in the simulation return home. I will leave that decision to you and Corduroy and Gold, if that becomes the case."

"This feels all too familiar, doesn't it?" Corduroy said sadly, from where he sat behind his desk. Velvet hadn't realised he was there.

"Atlantis?" she said softly.

Corduroy nodded. "Sabotaging the machine that was created so that we could live forever. The machine then imploding and destroying our world." He closed his eyes and sighed. "And so the cycles continue."

Velvet wanted to comfort her friend, but she had no idea what to say. It did indeed feel very familiar, as yet again, it was down to her to save as many as she could from the impending doom. She just hoped that she would not have to sacrifice herself to do so this time.

She took a deep breath and addressed the room again.

"My dear friends, though I am so very glad to have you here, I must stress that this is entirely voluntary. You are not required to go, and so if you should decide to return home now, you are free to do so with no fear of judgment. You will always have my love and gratitude." No one moved, and Velvet smiled. "Very well, if we could all join hands, and then concentrate on ourselves as we were in 2023, I will tune into Bk who is operating the machine, and he will do the rest." She clasped Amethyst's right hand in her left, and Aria's tiny left hand in her right.

"Good luck, Earth Angels. Peace, love and light be with you always."

# CORDUROY

## CHAPTER NINE

"I just think that if I could give it another go, I could finally resolve the issues with my dad, and maybe even have a relationship that isn't so toxic, you know? Well, hmm, it might take more than one go, but I think that I could do a better job in the next loop, I really do. After all, I'm pretty sure that in the last loop, it was the first time that my dad had ever said 'I love you' to me without being prompted, which is-"

"Wait," Corduroy said, holding up his hand, stopping the woman mid-ramble. "What did you say just then?"

The woman, who was his first one-to-one session for the day, frowned. "My dad said 'I love you' without being prompted?"

Corduroy looked at his notes and shook his head to himself. "Haven't you told me this before?"

"No," the woman said slowly. "This is our first session, I only returned from Earth yesterday. When would I have told you this?"

Corduroy knew she was telling the truth, his blank notes and schedule confirmed it, but something in his gut didn't feel right. He was having a major case of déjà vu, and that was not usually a good thing. He could have sworn that he had experienced this exact session before, in fact - "Were you about to say that if only your father could have told you when you were younger that he loved you, that you might have taken a different path sooner? That you would have found your purpose and then you wouldn't have got addicted to alcohol?" he asked, not knowing where the information was coming from, but judging from the look on her face, it was correct.

"Er, yeah, how did you know that? Have you got my record or something?"

Corduroy shook his head. "No, I'm sorry, can we resume this tomorrow? I need to figure something out."

The woman nodded and left his office, still looking quite confused.

Corduroy didn't blame her. He was quite confused himself. What in the world was going on? He checked in with himself, and found that he had an extra layer of fatigue to his body that wasn't normally there. And he felt... stuck? Quite the odd feeling to have, when he was busy every day with different humans, helping them to return to the loop to try to evolve further. He sighed and tucked his notes away, wondering if he should consult with Bk. They weren't due to meet for a catch up until the next day, but seeing as he now had a spare hour until his next session, he felt the urge to seek the Starperson out, and see if he knew what was causing the déjà vu.

He got up from his desk and crossed the hall to the operations room, where he knew he would most likely find Bk, working hard, no doubt. Starpeople rarely rested.

The door disappeared to admit him, and as he had

predicted, Bk was seated at the console, staring up at the hundred screens all showing information that was complete nonsense to Corduroy. He would never understand it, never in a million years.

"Bk," he said. "How are things?" He didn't want to dive right in with his confusion, it felt too strange to confide in Bk when they usually only exchanged pleasantries and strategies.

Bk looked up, surprised to see the Head of the Academy in his office. He shook his head as though to ground himself. "Corduroy? This is... unscheduled. What's wrong?"

Corduroy chuckled. He should have known better than to try and keep anything from a light being who picked up on nonverbal cues. "I'm not sure? But something feels, um, a little off? I was in a one-to-one, and I had the strongest feeling of-"

"Déjà vu?" Bk asked.

Corduroy nodded and took the seat next to Bk at the console. "Yes. I knew exactly what she was going to say, in fact, I felt like I had already heard her words a thousand times before, not just the once. How is that possible? I am not a Seer. But something is not right."

Bk sighed. "You are right there. Something is most definitely not right. I have been trying to analyse the data we received from all the dimensions we are in contact with, and just like you, I feel as though I have read the same data over and over, that I can almost predict it, with startling accuracy."

"So what is going on?" Corduroy asked. "Why is this happening?"

Bk shook his head and looked up at the screens. "I honestly don't know, I mean, the data is all normal, it's just that I feel that I have seen it before. It doesn't make sense."

"Okay," Corduroy said, getting up to pace back and forth, as he often did when trying to fathom out a problem. "We are both experiencing déjà vu, but feel as though we have experienced the same thing multiple times, not just the once before, which would suggest that perhaps..."

"We are in a loop?" Bk said thoughtfully.

"Is the machine in good working order?" Corduroy asked. He had never seen the machine before, he only knew of its existence, he had hoped to see it, but didn't trust himself to be near something so powerful, his long distant past still haunted him.

Bk glanced at the back of the office. "I haven't checked it today, but it was fine yesterday, and there's been no warnings come up," he waved at the screen in the far left hand corner. "But seeing as we are looking for anything weird, I will run a few diagnostics, and get back to you."

Corduroy nodded. "Thank you, yes that would be good. I will be in my office, do come and let me know if you find anything out of the ordinary. Make this a priority for today?"

"Of course," Bk said, hitting a few buttons to close the programs he had running on the screens. "I'm on it."

Corduroy left the office, glancing back just in time to see Bk disappear through a secret door at the back of the office. He sighed. If only he could trust himself. But the idea of delving too deep into a technology beyond his skill was a temptation too great to resist.

He just hoped that Bk could make sense of their predicament, because it felt like alarm bells were ringing loudly now, and he was feeling quite unnerved. It took quite a lot to unnerve him, he was the former Professor of

Death, after all.

*   *   *

Corduroy was immersed in reading his notes for his next session when he heard a noise in front of him. He glanced up and swore loudly.

"Bk! Why are you sneaking up on me like that? I'd have had a heart attack if I were still human!"

Bk held his finger to his lips and held up a small screen to show Corduroy, which said simply -

*Follow Me.*

Corduroy started to say something but Bk shook the screen and it now said -

*Quietly.*

Frowning but complying, Corduroy got up and silently followed Bk out of the room. He expected to go to the operations room, but Bk went the opposite way, towards the main hall. But he didn't stop there, he kept going until they reached the outer doors to the Academy. The doors were rarely used, as no one really arrived and entered through them, they were simply transported to the main hall. Feeling slightly impatient but very curious, Corduroy kept following Bk until he took an abrupt right turn and walked along the edge of the mists around the Academy.

At a seemingly random spot, Bk turned to Corduroy and pointed at the wall. Corduroy looked at the gleaming white outer wall of the Academy and frowned. He couldn't see anything. He shrugged to show his confusion, and Bk motioned for him to reach out to touch it. Corduroy reached out and found that his hand struck something quite solid before it reached the wall. He put both hands out and felt the invisible object. It appeared to be quite small, and somehow attached to the wall. And if he listened hard, he could hear a slight buzzing. He turned to Bk and mouthed "What is it?" He still had no idea why they had to be quiet.

Bk shook the screen again and now it said - *StarTech*.

*Well that's as clear as mud*, Corduroy thought, feeling more impatient than curious now.

Bk reached out to take his arm, and then clicked his fingers, transporting them both instantly back to Corduroy's office.

"I'm sorry to be so weird," Bk whispered once they were seated at the desk. "I'm worried that we are being listened to, but there's no way to be sure. Basically, the Academy has been infiltrated, and put in a time loop. The device you could feel but not see is a piece of StarTech that blocks any outside communication to and from the Academy. We have been cut off from the outside realms."

"Okay," Corduroy said slowly. "What does that mean? Where has it come from? Who put it there?"

Bk shook his head. "I don't know yet, I'm still running diagnostics, but well, it doesn't feel like they are friendly."

"They're from your planet though if you recognise the tech? I thought you guys were pretty benign."

Bk shrugged "We are, or, well, were. Who knows what has happened in the eons since I left?"

"So what does this mean? We are in a loop? Like Earth? Is that what is causing the déjà vu?"

Bk nodded uncomfortably. "Yes, but well, Earth is in a loop of about a hundred years, and our loop here? It's only a day."

Corduroy's eyes widened. "A day?" he hissed. "How many times have we lived the same day?"

Bk gulped. "Approximately eight thousand times."

"EIGHT THOUSAND?" Corduroy yelled while Bk waved madly at him to be quiet. "What the actual...? Are you certain?"

Bk nodded. "Yes, the Starperson hacked into the machine and though they could have looped up to a month or more, they set it to a day."

Corduroy got up and started pacing up and down. "So we have lived the same day over and over for the last-"

"Twenty-three years," Bk confirmed.

Corduroy stopped in his tracks and closed his eyes. "Well no wonder I feel so damned tired." He started pacing again. "So clearly, whoever did this wanted us out of action, but why? Have you been able to get hold of Gold?"

"He was called to the Angelic Realm, so he is not at his post, I tried to get a message through to the Angels but it seems that their realm is blocked. I suspect more of the same tech, same person."

"Are they looped too?"

"I couldn't find a loop for them, but the tech blocking them might have also frozen them in time."

"Shit. What do we do?"

"Whatever we do, it has to be today. Tomorrow, it will be this morning again and we will have no memory of this."

Corduroy sat down heavily in his chair and sighed. "And we will be stuck in this day for goodness knows how long. Okay, how long will the diagnostics take on the machine?"

"Another few hours? It's a lot of data to process." Bk looked as weary as Corduroy felt. "But I don't think we should wait until we have the full picture. We need to release Gold and the Angels, and the Academy, from this eternal day."

"And you can do that? You can stop the machines blocking us, and stop our loop?"

"The machine here will only take a few moments to deactivate, which we will have to do before we can leave." Bk sighed. "The loop is easy to stop, but I just haven't yet because I didn't know if it was for the best. I mean, I don't know what will happen to everyone at the Academy, they might be suddenly transported to where they should be right now." He shrugged. "It's tricky to tell what will happen when you mess with time."

Corduroy sighed. "Okay, let's visit the Angelic Realm, unblock them, and then see how Gold wants to play it." He got up and went around the desk to Bk, took his arm and then clicked his fingers.

# CHAPTER TEN

"Wow, that really did only take you moments to dismantle," Corduroy commented as Bk took apart the invisible tech that had kept the Angelic Realm cut off from the outside realms.

"Yeah it had a built in barrier to stop anyone leaving too, so even if they had known what was happening, they wouldn't have been able to get out to do anything about it," Bk said, examining the device he had just disabled.

"The hour grows late," Corduroy commented. "We had better find Athena, Pallas and Gold and explain the situation before we get reset."

Bk tucked the device into a bag he manifested with the click of his fingers and then followed Corduroy to the gates, where Pearl was stood, looking visibly upset.

"Pearl," Corduroy called out. "Are you well?"

Pearl saw the Old Soul and the Starperson and burst into tears. "Oh, Corduroy! I'm so glad you are here, I don't know what is going on. I feel like I have been stuck for such a long time, I couldn't move! Couldn't walk, talk or enter the Realm, until just a few moments ago! What in heaven's name is going on?”

Corduroy wasn’t a fan of hugs, but he couldn’t help but gather the Angel into his arms while she calmed down. He thought it had been bad enough, trapped in the same day over and over for twenty years, but to be stuck in suspended animation with no way out? He couldn’t imagine anything more horrific. What kind of cruel being could have done this to such a beautiful Angel?

“Oh, Pearl, I am so very sorry. We came the moment we worked out there was an issue. We were stuck in a loop, we had no idea what was happening,” Bk said.

Corduroy released the Angel, and she waved her hand at the gate which opened and she accompanied them into the realm, which was in a state of complete and utter chaos. Corduroy couldn’t quite comprehend the scene they were met with.

Angels were running and flying in all directions, the distress was evident in their frantic calls for each other.

“Were they all stuck in time, like Pearl?” Corduroy muttered to Bk. “Not even a loop of a day, but just frozen?”

Bk looked around the golden realm and nodded grimly. “Judging by their states of being, I would guess so, yes.”

“Goddess almighty,” Corduroy muttered. “Let’s find Gold, and explain what we know to him.”

Bk nodded and they followed Pearl to the main building where there was a flurry of Angels all clamouring to know what was going on. A few of them noticed the Starperson and the Old Soul and the whispering began, as they wondered what was happening and why they were there.

“Corduroy!”

The Old Soul looked up to see Gold striding towards him, and he sighed in relief. Gold would know what to do.

"Gold, are you okay? Have you been stuck all this time?"

Gold reached them and motioned for them to join him inside, away from the whispering Angels.

Once they were inside, Corduroy could see Pallas and Athena in a frantic discussion.

"We know why you were all stuck," Corduory said, diving right in. He was still aware that he and Bk could get reset at any point, it was now very late in the day, though he didn't know if the machine loop could still affect them as they were not within the walls of the Academy. "There was a device just outside the gates which paused time in the realm, effectively freezing you all in the moment you were in."

"Where did the device come from?" Athena demanded. "Who put it there?"

"How long have we been frozen?" Pallas asked at the same time.

Bk answered them. "We believe it to be a Starperson, due to the tech used. We too were frozen in time, though we were put in a loop, and lived the same day over and over. We have not worked out who the Starperson is yet though."

"How long?" Pallas repeated, fear in her usually calm and hopeful eyes.

"Twenty-three Earthly years," Corduroy answered.

She slumped backwards into the gold brocaded chair behind her, while Athena gasped, her hand flying to her face. Gold just groaned.

"To what end?" he asked. "What was their plan?"

Corduroy shook his head. "We do not know. Bk has been running diagnostics on the machine to see what has happened to the Earth loop, to see if it has been impaired in any way. It feels as though the Starperson was seeking some kind of revenge? We are not really sure at this stage. The day loop at the Academy is still active. Bk can stop it, but we wished to seek your advice first, on what will happen to those at the Academy if we do so."

Gold sighed. "I have absolutely no idea, I'm afraid. You will just have to stop it and find out. Perhaps gather all the beings into one place, that way, you can see if any of them disappear? I'm sorry that I have no wisdom for you."

Bk nodded. "I figured that may be the case. And as such, we cannot expect wisdom when you have been trapped in a single moment for over twenty years."

Gold nodded. "It felt like an eternity, to be honest, and I have battled the whole time with myself and my thoughts, with wondering what was happening and whether it was ever going to end."

"I'm so sorry, Gold. And to you, Athena, Pallas. So very sorry."

"Oh, Bk," Athena said, getting up to hug the Starperson. "You are not to blame, it was not you who did this to us."

Bk pulled away, looking ashamed. "But it was my kin. And they used my tech that I left on Zubenelgenubi eons ago. I may not have planted these devices, but I did create them. So I am responsible."

"In which case, I'm sure you will help us to rectify this situation quickly," Gold said. "I will accompany you both back to the Academy, and we shall see what can be done." He turned to the two Head Guardian Angels. "Athena, Pallas, gather the Angels and explain the situation to them, get them searching Earth and the rest of the universe for the soul responsible, and perhaps we can bring them to justice."

The two Angels nodded, pulling themselves together in order to carry out their orders.

Corduroy and Bk nodded farewell to the Angels, then followed Gold to the gates. The Angels outside parted to allow them through, and when they went beyond the gates, they both held Gold's arms and he clicked his fingers.

*   *   *

"Apologies for the disruption to your evening," Corduroy said to the assembled Academy students in the main hall. "But there has been a situation, and I needed to gather you all here while we try to resolve it. If you can all just be seated, we are just going to have a few moments of quiet, then we can discuss."

There was a few moments of noise and movement as the students all found seats, then once settled and quiet, Corduroy muttered "Bk, Bk, Bk."

"Yes, I'm at the machine," Bk replied in Corduroy's ear.

"All students are in the main hall, I am watching to see if anything shifts," Corduroy whispered under his breath, so that none in the front row could hear him.

"Okay, disabling the loop now."

Corduroy sucked in a deep breath, steeling himself for what might happen in the next few moments. Would the students disappear? Would he? Would he suddenly be in a different dimension?

The moments ticked by, and the students began whispering amongst themselves, Corduroy shifted about impatiently in his seat. Was it done yet?

"Well?" he whispered.

"This is a bit trickier than I thought it would be, I need a few more moments," Bk replied.

Corduroy nodded even though Bk wouldn't be able to

see that.

Feeling tense but at the same time, absolutely exhausted, Corduroy found himself closing his eyes for a moment, needing to calm himself.

"Corduroy? Are you okay?"

The Old Soul jolted awake with a start, looking up at Bk and Gold who were stood on the stage next to the chair where he sat. He looked down at the seats to see that they were empty, and he sighed.

"They're gone," he said. "Where did they go?"

Gold shrugged. "Onward. They were never meant to be here for that long. They must have been called onward the moment the loop was broken." He paused, deep in thought. "Or perhaps they returned to their Earthly bodies. We may never know."

Corduroy sighed. "Well I suppose at least we don't have to worry about them now, let's just hope they are where they should be. So what's next?"

"The diagnostics should have finished, I left Dahlia in charge of compiling the results, let's see what she has."

The three men joined hands and Bk took them back to the operations room with a click.

The moment they arrived, Corduroy winced at the sound of wailing.

"Dahlia, what is it?" Bk asked, rushing over to the console where the pink Faerie with dragonfly wings was wailing. She was crying too hard to respond, but waved her hand at the screens before her, which were covered in symbols that Corduroy could not comprehend.

But Bk could. A few moments later, he was shaking his head as his eyes flew back and forth across the screens. "Oh, no," he whispered.

"Bk?" Corduroy said, not sure he really wanted to know what the symbols meant. Gold was also studying the screens, and his face looked like it had aged another eon in the last few moments.

"Oh goddess," he said. "This is... this is bad."

"Bad?" Bk hissed. "That's the understatement of the millennium."

"Can someone please explain?" Corduroy demanded of the sound of the pink Faerie still wailing. His patience had all but gone, and as much as he was afraid to know he hated being the last.

Bk looked at him. "The Earth loop has been destroyed."

Corduroy frowned. "Okay? What does that mean? Has Earth ended? No more humans now?"

Bk shook his head. "No, not quite, look, I can show you." Bk turned and headed for the secret door, motioning for Corduroy to follow him. Despite the gravity of the situation, Corduroy felt a flicker of excitement at being allowed to see the secret machine at long last.

He followed Bk into the tiny back room, amazed at the incredible piece of tech that was hidden within it. He sat in the chair that Bk held out for him, and with a few buttons pressed, a holographic image flickered to life in front of him, and he was shown exactly what the situation on Earth was, and how things had been over the previous twenty-three years.

When the screen went blank and the light flickered out, he looked at Bk in horror.

"Shit."

# CHAPTER ELEVEN

The three men had been sitting in silence in Corduroy's office for some time before Bk finally cleared his throat and spoke up.

"I will do my best to try and undo the damage, but the hack is too good. I think all traces of the Diamond Age have been removed, including the back-ups. The only path that exists for humans on Earth now is the one they are currently experiencing."

"Which means that it will soon end in pain and darkness?" Corduroy enquired, his voice flat.

"Worse," Bk said, his own voice devoid of life. "The Earth will be destroyed, which means that there will be an impact on other planets."

There was more silence. Corduroy didn't know what to say. He didn't even really fully understand the technology, or understand how the looping worked. How could he possibly devise a solution?

"We need to find the Starperson responsible, and get them to reverse the hack," Gold said. "We have the Angels looking for them, but I don't assume it will be easy to recognise them? That is, of course, assuming that they are currently on Earth."

"I assume that's where they are too," Bk said. "So they can witness the chaos they have created. I know they haven't gone home because I found their ship hidden in the docking station."

Corduroy looked up at Bk. "You did? You didn't say."

Bk nodded. "After I disabled the device, I had a scout around. It's there, clear as day. Well, if you have the ability to see invisible flying ships."

"So we need people on the ground, as it were. We need Earth Angels on Earth, conscious and searching for the Starperson." Corduroy sighed. "I can go. I wasn't there during this particular reality, but I can be a walk-in? Just appear on Earth as Pearl and the other Angels did?"

Bk shook his head. "No can do, the walk-in program has been destroyed."

Corduroy swore. "Damned aliens." He closed his eyes and sighed. "Sorry, Bk."

"It's okay. I'm pretty frustrated right now too. That my tech has been used in this way... I want to get them too. But we are going to need Earth Angels who existed in this reality to go back there. To become awake and aware in their bodies again."

Corduroy tapped his fingers on his brown wooden desk, while his brain whirred through the possibilities. But it didn't take long for a crystal clear image of the right person to come into his mind. He looked up at Gold, who nodded as though in response to his thoughts.

"Velvet," Gold confirmed. "She is the only one for the job."

Corduroy sighed. It took a considerable amount of effort

for his dearest old love not to be in his mind constantly. He still held a torch for her, still longed for her touch. Even after their disastrous relationship on Earth and the fact that she had spent the last few eons with her Flame.

"I hate to ask her," he said. "She created heaven on Earth, and now we have to tell her it was destroyed? So now she has to save the world, again?"

"I will go," Gold said. "She should hear it from me. But this time, I will not force her to do anything. If she won't come, then we will have to rethink."

Corduroy sighed. "She will come. She won't be able to resist." He looked around his office, remembering how it was when Velvet was the head of the Academy. It wasn't so different back then, just the colour of the furniture and the additional desk for Linen, as well as the piano. It was plainer now. With the white walls and minimal brown furnishings. He tried not to allow himself to get lost in the memory of his old love. It wouldn't help him now. Especially when he was potentially about to see her again.

"I will keep working on the machine in the meantime," Bk said, standing up to leave. "Perhaps there is a fix I have yet to consider." He nodded to the Old Soul and the Elder and left the room.

"She won't be pleased to see you," Corduroy said.

Gold chuckled. "She is never pleased to see me." He tilted his head thoughtfully at the Old Soul. "I feel that you will be pleased to see her though? I thought that having spent a life with your Flame, your love for Velvet would have abated."

Corduroy sighed. "After the reboot, I didn't call my Flame to me. She is still in one of the higher dimensions, carrying out her purpose. She doesn't remember me, I don't think. I visited her once, just to see, and she didn't know me."

"So you let her go," Gold said.

"Yes."

"But not Velvet, how interesting. I do find this business of soulmates and Twin Flames fascinating, don't you?"

Corduroy shook his head. "No, not particularly. I could certainly live without feeling like there's a part of me missing."

Gold nodded. "How well I know that feeling. Anyway," he stood up and bowed his head slightly. "I shall get on my way to the Seventh, and hope that your old love is willing to help us."

"I wish you well, Gold. I hope to see you soon."

Gold clicked his fingers and disappeared, a small cloud of gold dust lingering in the space he had just occupied.

Corduroy realised then that they hadn't discussed what he would do while they were on their missions. With no humans now at the Academy, Corduroy had no daily routine or tasks. It seemed that all he could do now, was wait.

*   *   *

Corduroy was on his fifth circuit of the gardens when he received a call from Bk. He paused mid-step. "Yes, Bk?"

"I think you need to see this," Bk said in his ear. "I'm in the hidden room."

Without a second thought, Corduroy clicked his fingers and reappeared at Bk's side in front of the machine in the hidden room. "What is it?" He was feeling frustrated and impatient, being left out of the action, and was thrilled to be a part of it. Even if Bk was going to show him something he wish he hadn't.

Bk looked up from the machine at the Old Soul. "I've found a hidden message, from another Starperson, and in it he identifies our hacker."

Corduroy's eyes widened. This was definitely a good development. "Who is it?"

"Au," Bk said with a sigh. "I remember her. She was a feisty spirit, always rebelling against the natural order of our planet."

"Okay, so we have a rogue alien in charge. Who left the message? She has an accomplice?"

Bk pressed a button and a holographic image appeared, and when Bk hit another button, it played like a video.

"Bk, I hope you get this, I really don't have much time, but something bad is about to go down, really bad. I was in another dimension when I felt a pull on my consciousness that was in the Earth loop, so I came back to my body to find that a Starperson called Au is trying to sabotage the machine and destroy humans. She's pissed that Zubenelgenubi is dead, and she thinks humans are to blame. She hasn't realised that I am back properly in my body, so I am playing along as though I'm just a duplicate, so that I can try to stop her, but I don't know if I will be able to, she is very determined."

Corduroy watched the video, recognising the soul in it. "That's Tm," he said. "He was a student here, in all realities, including the reboot. But he lived through the Diamond Age, how did he come back here?"

As if he could hear Corduroy's question, Tm continued.

"Au orchestrated my death and then recruited me to help her. She plans to take me back to Earth with her as a walk-in, where we will recruit other Starpeople and create a hell on Earth. She wants humans to suffer as much as she has. The thing is, I don't think it will take much effort on her part, you know what humans are like. It took so much effort to get them into the Diamond Age, to a time of peace, love and support for every soul. I hate to imagine what she will be able to do. And I will do my best to resist, but she is very convincing in her arguments." Tm looked to the side then and made a face. "I have to go, she's coming back. I will try to record more later about her plans."

The holograph flickered out and Corduroy looked at Bk. "Was there more?"

Bk shook his head. "No, that was it. Seems he didn't get the chance to record anymore."

"Damn. Would have been good to get more intel. But let's see, what do we have?"

Bk held up a hand. "One, we know her identity. Two, we know her motivations, she wants revenge for her home being destroyed, Three, we know the identity of the first Starperson she recruited. Four, she wants to recruit more. Five, she planned to create hell on Earth."

Corduroy waved his hand at the machine. "Judging by what you showed me, I would say she has successfully completed that mission. Earth is a mess, and Tm was right, it probably didn't take much effort. I know very well how dark humans can be. They barely need an excuse to become killing machines."

Bk put his hand on Corduroy's shoulder. "This is good, we have a better idea of what we are looking at, of who we are looking for. This will be useful for when Velvet gets here. I have already relayed the information to Gold, in case he needs it to persuade her."

"Is he with her now?"

Bk chuckled. "He delayed getting to her for a while, pretending it was because of the difficulty of travelling to the Seventh, but really I know that he just sat in the Atlantis Garden for a while. It was receiving my message that then prompted him to go."

Corduroy frowned. "I didn't see him there on my walk."

Bk laughed harder. "Yeah he hid in the bushes every time you passed. It was quite amusing to watch."

Corduroy laughed too. "I bet it was. Wait, you can see everything that's happening in the Academy? Are the recordings kept? Couldn't we look at the footage of when Au was here?"

"She destroyed it. She destroyed all the footage recorded prior to her leaving here with Tm. I had already checked that possibility."

"Of course you did, sorry." Corduroy pondered Tm's words. "Do you think he managed to change anything? It seems like the Earth is in a pretty terrible state right now. Do you think she finally managed to persuade him that they were doing the right thing?"

Bk shrugged. "Maybe. They were very close, as far as I can tell. Au, Tm and Mg. They started off as tiny sparks together, and were inseparable until Mg decided to leave for Earth. I left not long after him. And then it seems Tm left too, and Au was on her own."

"And so the bitterness grew," Corduroy mused. "I can understand that, at least."

"So it seems. Still no excuse for what she has done. I only hope that Velvet chooses to help us."

"She will," Corduroy said confidently, even though his stomach was flipping over at the thought of seeing her again. "I have absolute faith in her."

# CHAPTER TWELVE

A couple of days later, Corduroy sat in his office in the dark for some time after Velvet, Laguz and Gold had left. Velvet had gone to recruit her Earth Angel friends, Laguz had gone to see Bk, and Gold had gone to see the Elders, to discuss the coming mission.

Corduroy could still smell Velvet's scent on his robes from when he had hugged her. Somehow she always smelled of their many past lives as friends. Days spent outside in the sun, the saltiness of sea air, the sweet spiced vanilla of their favourite pastries.

He sighed. He could recall every moment spent in her company. Every moment of their many lifetimes as humans. Every single touch, whisper, laughter. But was any of it real? The machine creating the loop had taught him that reality was not the concrete absolute that he had once believed it was. Reality could be created, manipulated, changed, even erased entirely. What was real? Because reality certainly wasn't. And if there was nothing real, where did that leave him? What was his mission? If they managed to save Earth from destruction, again, what would that mean?

He frowned. Surely all they needed to do was destroy the machine? If the machine didn't exist, and the loop did not exist, then wouldn't Earth in fact, be saved? He really wished he actually understood the technology better. Because destroying the machine in Atlantis had not ended well for him, or anyone else, in fact. Except for Laguz. He let out another sigh, disgusted with himself for still holding such a grudge against his fishy-tailed foe.

Why couldn't he just be happy for his oldest friend? Because until she was wrenched out of her perfect existence and back here to deal with this galactic fuck-up, she had been very happy indeed. Living her long-awaited eternity with her Flame.

Unable to deal with his own ego anymore, he got up and left his office, going across to the operations room. It was unlikely that Bk hadn't already considered shutting down or destroying the machine, but he needed to at least make the suggestion, even though it did have a strong feeling of déjà vu attached to it. At least, this time, Corduroy was not rashly doing it himself, but seeking to discover the consequences of such actions first.

He stepped through the doorway and found the control room empty aside from Dahlia, who was concentrating on something on the screens.

"Hey," he said quietly, so as not to startle her. He knew she could be quite the jumpy Faerie. Despite his caution, she still jumped a mile, her wings fluttering as she caught herself in mid-air.

"Oh! Corduroy! You scared me. Are you okay?"

Corduroy smiled. "Yes, I was hoping to speak to Bk, is he in the machine room?"

Dahlia nodded and settled back in her chair.

Corduroy glanced at the screens where incomprehensible symbols were flying around. "Anything interesting?"

Dahlia looked up at him and nodded. "Just tracking Velvet's progress."

"Okay, good, if she needs any assistance, do let me know."

"Sure," Dahlia said, her attention turning back to the screens.

Corduroy moved to the back of the room, and stood where he thought the door was. He called Bk in his mind and asked for permission to enter. Part of the wall disappeared and he entered the room where Bk and Laguz were sat in front of the machine.

He greeted them both, though he couldn't look Laguz in the eyes. He relayed his ponderings on the idea of stopping the loop and turning off the machine, and he heard a grunt of disbelief from Laguz, forcing Corduroy to look at his face.

"Are you serious?" Laguz asked. "I guess you never did change. How can you think that destroying the machine would help? What would happen to all of the souls in loop?"

Corduroy thought of all his students sitting in the main hall before him, disappearing when Bk had dismantled the day loop they had been trapped in. He dropped his head. "They would most likely disappear. The humans would be taken onward, and any conscious Earth Angels would go home to their dimensions, or to wherever they chose."

"But you don't know that for sure though, do you? What if they cease to exist entirely?" Laguz's tone irritated Corduroy, even though he knew he was right. Because the truth was, Corduroy didn't know for sure. He had no idea where his students had gone. He was just trying to be optimistic. For the first time in his very long existence.

"It's not a terrible idea," Bk said. "But Au has managed to disable the machine in such a way that a reboot is not possible. We would have to actually dismantle the machine. And I honestly have no idea what that would do to those within the loop, or even to us, or to the universe. The ripples could be bad, but I honestly don't know."

Corduroy nodded. "It was just a thought. I figured you would have already considered it, but at this point, all ideas have to be on the table?"

Bk nodded, but Laguz didn't look convinced.

The was a moment of silence and Corduroy shuffled his feet awkwardly, feeling like Laguz and Bk were just waiting for him to leave so they could continue whatever they were doing.

"Right, well, I'll be in my office if you need me," he muttered. He hated feeling useless and unnecessary. He clicked his fingers to return to his office quickly, not giving them a chance to respond.

He sat heavily in his chair at his desk, feeling completely exhausted, but knowing that sleep would not be coming any time soon.

*　*　*

"Corduroy!"

Corduroy jumped in his seat and looked up from his desk to see Magenta entering his office. He couldn't help but smile widely. It seemed that Velvet had indeed worked her magic.

"Magenta," Corduroy said, getting up to greet the Seer. "You came."

Magenta smiled. "Of course, how could I not?"

Corduroy embraced the Old Soul. "It was a big ask. But Velvet is very persuasive."

Magenta released him and chuckled. "So that's why you sent her?" She looked around the empty office. "I'm the first to arrive?"

Corduroy manifested a chair for her with a click of his fingers and then sat on the edge of his desk. "We asked Velvet to do this mission because she was the only one we thought could."

"Undoubtedly. There is no one else in the universe with her influence and friendships." Magenta sighed. "That a soul that was once benevolent could cause such chaos and destruction..." she shook her head. "The darkness must have really destroyed their light."

Corduroy shrugged. "I'm surprised it took them this long. They had been on their planet in darkness for a considerable length of time. A human wouldn't have taken that long to reach the point of retribution. I'm only sorry that we were unable to stop them."

"You were trapped in a single day for twenty-three years?" Magenta inquired.

Corduroy nodded. "Yes, it was a version of hell to be sure, but we were unaware of our situation. Whereas the Angelic Realm were frozen in a moment for that time, but were entirely aware. Now that is a definite kind of hell."

Magenta shook her head. "And none of us had any idea, in the other dimensions. To be honest, I didn't even realise that the Academy had continued, that the Earth loop existed. Whose idea was that?"

Corduroy cleared his throat, went to sit in his chair then shifted about uncomfortably. "Ah, yeah, that might have been mine. I had no idea it was possible when I made the suggestion though. It was Bk that made it possible with modifications and upgrades to his machine."

Magenta tutted but didn't say anything, which made Corduroy feel awful.

"I know, I know. If the loop didn't exist, if Earth had been left fallow, then none of this would be happening now. I'm aware of this and feel suitably awful. If I could turn back the clock, I would. But I can't, because that part of the machine has been disabled in a way that Bk cannot override."

Magenta smiled. "I didn't say anything."

"You didn't need to," he muttered.

Magenta's gaze shifted to the side of his left shoulder and he frowned. "What is it?"

Magenta's gaze slid back to his face and she smiled again. "The others are here, and Velvet will be back soon."

Corduroy nodded and stood up, ready to greet them. He tried to shake off the blame and judgement he had felt from Magenta, and focus on the task at hand. He was going to make up for his bad ideas and decisions, and get that rebellious alien back there to fix the mess, even if it was the last thing he ever did.

# Aria

## Chapter Thirteen

When Aria opened her eyes and looked around, it took her a full minute to work out where she was.

Or even *who* she was.

She sat up suddenly as her memories came flooding back, wincing as they crashed around her mind, fighting with the memories stored in the brain of the body she now inhabited. Her Earthly body, the one she had not been in since the Diamond Age. Her weak, wingless, human body.

She jumped out of bed and immediately groaned. She had forgotten how heavy and miserable human bodies were. The aches and pains alone were enough to make her rethink her rash decision to come back. But Velvet was depending on her.

She surveyed the bedroom, and noted that it was different to last time. There was a single bed, for starters. But wasn't it the 2020s? Shouldn't she have a partner? Maybe time had been changed so that she and Tm had never met? She supposed that made sense, but how come she hadn't met anyone else?

She went to the door and ripped it open, only to be

confronted with the sight of a half-naked woman walking past.

"Oh, morning, Anna," the woman mumbled with a yawn. "Don't mind if I go to the bathroom first?"

Aria shook her head, still in shock. She was in a shared house? She really was single?

She already hated this reality.

She had been told that Tm had been recruited by Au, but surely he would have come looking for her when he got there? She knew they weren't Flames, but they had once shared a human life together, built a home, and a family. Didn't he even try to seek her out?

She sighed. Maybe he had. But maybe she hadn't recognised him, because she hadn't woken up. Bk did mention something about the Star Program being compromised.

She retreated back into her room, and threw on some clothes. She needed to make a plan to find Tm, even though she had no idea how to do that. But if she did, the chances were that he would know how to find Au, and they could get this mess sorted out.

Oh, if only they had gone to the same dimensions after the Diamond Age. Instead, they had chosen separate missions to pursue, and chosen to reunite with their Flames. They had not seen each other in eons. Perhaps if they had met up more often, Aria would have noticed his absence, could have alerted everyone before it got this late. Twenty-three years of unchecked chaos created by a rogue alien seeking revenge? It was a plot more terrible than any doomsday movie she had ever watched in her last human life.

Once she was dressed, in a mismatched kaleidoscope of

colours, she jammed shoes on her feet and grabbed what she assumed was her phone. She needed food, and she needed to do some research.

"Tim," she muttered as she thundered down the stairs towards the kitchen. "I'm coming, Alien."

*   *   *

Three chocolate donuts, two cups of coffee, and an hour later, Aria was no closer to finding Tm. Where was the alien hiding? Or had Au covered his trail, because she knew that one day, Aria and the other Earth Angels would come for them? Maybe he had assumed a different identity, after all, he had walked in to this reality, rather than being born.

Aria slammed her phone down on the dining table in frustration.

"Wow, another dating disaster?" her housemate commented as she poured herself a cup of coffee. "You got home pretty late last night, I had assumed it had gone well."

Aria sighed. "No, I'm sure it was fine." She really didn't want to search her human memory for the night before. The idea of being with someone other than Tim or Linen gave her the shivers. But her housemate's comment on dating confirmed that she had no significant other. "Tell me, if you needed to find someone who didn't want to be found, where would you look?"

Her housemate lifted an eyebrow. "Er, been ghosted again? Because that usually means they're not interested."

Aria sighed. "No, I'm trying to track down an old friend, and I can't find any trace of him."

"Have you checked obituaries?"

Aria frowned. "I don't think he's dead. But he might

have changed his name..." Her eyes lit up suddenly. "That's it!" She grabbed her phone and began furiously searching for Tim instead of his human name, Tom. She got a hit almost immediately, and she knew that he had done it so that she would find him. She had always called him Tim.

"Okay dokie, glad to help." Her housemate drifted off, mug in hand, while Aria found Tim's profile on social media, and she smiled at the symbol he had used for his profile picture. It was their special symbol that they had created for a book series they co-wrote and illustrated. A book series that in this reality, never existed.

She opened up a chat box and thought for a moment. What if Au was monitoring his messages? She might still not know that he had awoken and was back in his human body. After a few moments of thought, she grinned. She typed in the message and hit send, hoping that she wouldn't have to wait too long for his reply.

*　　*　　*

When her phone pinged two hours later, Aria let out a whoop of joy when she saw Tim's name pop up on the screen.

"Finally!" She opened the message and read it, a smile spreading across her face. Despite the lack of detail in the message, she knew exactly what it meant. It was a shorthand that they had developed when they wrote together. Her eyes welled up with tears when she thought about the life that they'd had together, and how he hadn't forgotten her, even after all this time. She really did love the Alien. Even if he was helping the enemy.

But was he? Why would he leave these breadcrumbs for

her to find if he had really gone over to the dark side?

She checked the time and swore, she needed to scoot. She opened the map app and figured out where she was, and how long it would take her to get to the location Tim had indicated. She needed to leave as soon as possible.

She ran upstairs to her room, grabbed a few things and jammed them into a small shoulder bag hanging on the back of the door. She paused briefly in front of the mirror and considered her appearance. She grabbed the hairbrush from the dresser and tried to pull it through her snarled blonde hair, but after a few moments, she gave up and threw the brush down. She looked in the mirror again and shrugged. Tim had never worried what she looked like before, why would he start now?

She ran downstairs and out the front door, not bothering to stop to lock it, or to even check it was closed. Then with her phone in hand, she switched directions on, and ran down the street, following the robotic voice that was telling her to turn left and right.

When she arrived in the park, she was sweating and breathing hard, and wondering why her human self was so unfit. Didn't she ever dance?

She reached the right spot, where she and Tim had reunited. In another life, another reality, eons ago as she danced on the frosty grass. She spun around in circles, trying to spot her favourite alien.

"Still dancing, I see?" a voice said softly from behind her.

Aria spun around and launched herself into his arms, making him laugh as he squeezed her and spun her around in dizzying circles. When he finally set her down, she had the chance to look up into his face, and her eyes widened.

"Oh, Tim, are you okay? You don't look good."

Tim laughed. "I have missed your honesty, Aria, I really have." He sighed. "I'm so much better now that you are here."

As Aria reached up on her tip-toes and kissed him, memories of their life that had been erased came flooding back to her. Days spent hunched over a laptop, creating their books, lazy mornings in bed, drinking coffee. Even their life previous to that, when they were just friends. The kiss lasted several moments before she pulled away, and saw that Tim's face looked lighter already. "You remembered everything too, didn't you?" she whispered.

Tim nodded, a tear falling down his cheek. "I had hoped that I could call you here from the other realms, but I didn't know how. I found your human incarnation a few years ago, but she wasn't you, just an unconscious version. I knew then that my messages at the Academy had not been received, that the cavalry was not coming."

Aria smiled and wiped his tear away with her thumb. "It's okay, I'm here now. And it's not just me who is back. So is Velvet, Beryl, Magenta and others."

Tim closed his eyes and let out a sigh of relief. "Thank the stars. I thought I was all alone."

"Not anymore," Aria said, reaching up to kiss him again. "We're here now, I'm here now."

Tim nodded and held her tighter. "So what's the plan?"

Aria frowned. "We have to find Au. Bk has tried to undo the damage she did to the machine, but he can't. Our only hope is to get Au back to the Academy to undo the damage. Do you know where she is?"

Tim sighed. "No, I don't. She is like a chameleon, keeps changing her disguise, pulling the strings from behind the curtain. I have been tracking everything that I think she has been behind though, and who she may have recruited."

Aria nodded. "It's a good place to start. Let's try and find some of her recruits, and then we can get in touch with Velvet and the others. They are also searching for her. We have a rendezvous scheduled in a couple of days, so we can share our findings. Right now though, I could really eat something, this human body has been starving since I woke up. Have you got any chocolate?"

Tim chuckled and took her hand, guiding her down the path and out of the park. "Let me guess, you only had sugar for breakfast?"

Aria giggled. "I had three donuts."

Tim shook his head. "You know that's not really food right?"

"Of course it is! Best food in the universe!" Aria protested.

Tim laughed and Aria's insides melted at the sound. She glanced up at him and saw that his deeply lined face looked more relaxed already. It was as though the last few millennia had melted away, and they were having a lazy Sunday morning walk before brunch.

It was as though everything was right with the world again. Even though it was very far from it.

# CHAPTER FOURTEEN

Over a long lunch in a favourite café that magically did still exist, Tim explained everything that had happened. From the moment he had re-entered his body fully at the Academy, to when they had walked back onto Earth, back to the year 2000, to carry out Au's plan.

Aria realised then why he looked so much older that she had expected. He had lived for an extra twenty years.

"How did you manage to avoid your old self?" Aria asked with a frown. "Wait, I searched for you, your human name, but it didn't exist? How is that possible?"

Tim sighed. "Because Au wiped me out of the system. I was never born. Then Au created IDs for us, and after a short while, she gave me my mission and then left."

Aria shook her head. "What a crazy, complicated plot. Surely there were easier ways to get her revenge?"

Tim laughed and sipped his tea. "You would think? I mean, destroying the machine would surely have been the quickest and easiest option. Then there would be no humans, job done. But her resentment had been growing like a cancer for millennia. She wanted something bigger than to just wipe out humans. She wanted them to suffer. And to be honest, it didn't take much, I don't think, to derail the humans. Especially as all of the Earth Angels were unconscious, and their human bodies were just on autoplay, as it were."

"But if she actually went back in time, if this is the real reality from the time when we experienced the Diamond Age, why weren't all the Earth Angels pulled back into their bodies? What pulled you back into your body?"

Tim shook his head and stared off into the distance, as though trying to remember something from long ago, which, Aria supposed, it was. "I'm not sure if I can define it. It wasn't like when the Guardian Angels called us to our human bodies, that loud, insistent calling of our name. It was softer, yet just as insistent, I suppose, like a whisper, saying that something wasn't right. I was with my Flame in the Eighth Dimension and I told her that something felt off. That there was this weird thread, that I felt like if I grabbed hold of it, it would take me somewhere, and that it was important that I go." He looked back at Aria, his lined face sad. "She told me to go, that if it felt important, it must be, that she would be okay, and would await my return." He sighed. "If I had known then, I might have resisted longer. I was not ready to leave my Flame."

Aria reached out to touch his hand. "I didn't want to leave Linen either. But when I heard that a rogue alien was trying to destroy humans, and that you were somehow involved, I knew I had to. You would have done the same for me. And I knew that you wouldn't be fooled into doing dark things for her, that you would be working on a plan."

Tim smiled and gripped her hand in his. "Yes, I would have come for you. Linen understood?"

Aria nodded. "He is a pretty awesome fire Faerie, that one. He knew that I wouldn't be able to rest knowing that you were in trouble. That all humans were in trouble. He wanted to come too, but I told him I didn't need that kind of distraction. Plus, he was someone else in this reality. He was called Mikey, not Theo, and yeah, it all seemed too complicated."

Tim chuckled. "Oh, to have an easy life, eh?"

Aria grinned. "But that would be so boring!" She finished the last of her rosemary and feta courgette pancakes and slurped down her drink. "So what's next? Can I see all your research? Shall we figure out who to contact?"

Tim nodded and wiped his mouth with a napkin. "Sure, we can go back to mine. But I gotta warn you, I don't think it's going to be as easy to contact them as you hope."

Aria frowned. "Why is that?"

"Because these Starpeople that I think were recruited? They are billionaires. They are CEOs. They are important and influential people with a lot of money and zero time for the little people. I don't even know how we could possibly get in touch with them, there are so many layers of protection around them."

Aria's eyes lit up. "So it will be a challenge! Excellent! Let's go." She hopped up from her seat and Tim followed her, leaving the right amount of cash on the table for the bill.

Outside the café, Aria reached out to clasp his hand in hers, and looked up at him. "So then, left or right?"

*　*　*

Evening had fallen while Aria and Tim were absorbed in

reading through his research, which consisted of notebooks, papers, drawings and maps. He hadn't kept anything in a digital space for fear of Au finding out that he was plotting against her.

Aria set down the notebook she was reading and rubbed her eyes. "You weren't kidding. These people are very influential. And rich."

Tim reached over the desk where they sat to put the lamp on. "I know. Au gave them a lot of help, made sure that they were successful, became the influencers, the leaders. She needed them to be her puppets, to inflict as much damage on the world as possible."

Aria sighed. "How did no one notice the huge shift in technology in the year 2000? I mean, it was an incredibly big jump, from the basic tech to the tech that is now possible. In the original reboot, the shift was softer. Technology didn't take over the world, people didn't lose the ability to communicate in person, they kept their connections and they didn't become addicted to screens. But in this reality…" Aria shook her head. "Are we too late? Is Earth doomed?"

Tim closed his eyes and leant back in his chair. "Maybe." A tear slid down his cheek and he opened his eyes to look at Aria. "But I tried," he whispered. "I tried to call the Earth Angels here, I tried to convince Au that this was a mistake. I even tried to convince her that we should go home to Zubenelgenubi, and revive it."

Aria grabbed Tim's hand and squeezed it. "No one is blaming you for this. Of course you have done your best." She frowned as something occurred to her. "Did you consider going home by yourself? To try and break the loop at the Academy?"

"I considered it," Tim said. "But I knew that Au had

planted tech to block communications in and out of the Academy, and in the Angelic Realm. I wasnt confident I could have dealt with the tech, so I thought it would be better to stay here. But I think maybe I was wrong."

Aria shook her head and waved her hand at all of the paperwork spread out before them. "But you have never given up. You have kept trying, kept going. I don't think I would have had as much faith as you. I think you were right to stay."

"I just don't see how we can change things now, too much has been set in motion, and I think that she has something big planned, I think the pandemic in 2020 was just the beginning."

Aria gulped. She hadn't dug around in her memories of that time, but she had watched the replay while at the Academy, and it had looked pretty awful to her. Something bigger than a global pandemic planned? She shuddered at the thought. "Well we can take all of this to the others when we meet them, and maybe they will have some ideas. Velvet will know what to do, I'm sure of it. She always knows what to do." Aria picked the notebook up again and continued reading Tim's neat shorthand.

"I hope you're right, Faerie," Tim sighed. "I really hope you're right."

* * *

"Tim! It's so good to see you!"

Aria grinned as Velvet hugged Tim. They had met up in a park a couple of hours away, and to the untrained eye, it would have looked like a bunch of friends meeting up for a picnic. Not a group of Angels, Faeries, Starpeople and Old

Souls, who were desperately trying to save the world.

Aria hugged Magenta and Beryl, and once the reintroductions were made (she had forgotten what some of them looked like in their human forms) the group sat on blankets on the grass in the sunshine, sharing food they had brought and catching up with developments that had occurred since they had arrived back on Earth.

Aria stuffed some olives in her mouth, and grabbed a hunk of bread and smothered it in cheese. Her human body was even more ravenous than her Faerie body, she just couldn't seem to stop eating.

"Thank you so much, all of you, for coming to Earth," Tim said, looking around the group. "I only wish that I had more for you than just my research, but I haven't been able to make any big changes." He sighed. "I also don't know where Au is right now. I just have this feeling that she has something big planned, but I don't know what it is." He pulled out a new notebook that he and Aria had been filling in longhand. They had written down the main points that needed to be considered, and the list of potential recruits that Au had working for her.

Velvet looked at the list. "I recognise some of these names, they were influential in the Diamond Age too, but they didn't take things to the extreme that they have now."

"Influential and also super rich and famous and untouchable," Aria said, popping a pickled onion in her mouth. "Yeah we have done some digging to see if we can get anywhere near them, but it looks pretty impossible."

"Are they all Starpeople?" Magenta asked. Velvet nodded and handed her the list.

"Yes, and all Zubenelgenubians, it seems. I suppose it was probably easy enough to convince them to help her, once she explained that their home was destroyed."

Tim cleared his throat. "Actually, she didn't plan to tell them that. She took on the guise of a wealthy investor, and just encouraged them to realise their wildest dreams. Being unconscious, but having the knowledge of our technology, it wasn't difficult for them to comply. Especially as they had no star download, and they forgot that they were meant to ease up on the tech, so that humans didn't forget how to communicate with one another."

Amethyst gasped, her hand flying to her heart. "That's it," she whispered.

Everyone stared at her, waiting for her to elaborate, but it was Aria who spoke up impatiently after a minute of silence.

"What? What is it?" she asked, nervously tearing off another bit of bread.

Amethyst looked around each of the group. "We need to make them conscious again, or we need to get them the star download. If we can't physically contact them here, we need to find them in the other dimensions and make them conscious again. Maybe if they could see what was going on, they could change things, and try to undo the damage."

Velvet raised her eyebrows. "That could work, although we have no idea where they might be."

"You found us," Beryl said. "It must be possible to find them too."

"I tuned into your energies though," Velvet said thoughtfully. "I don't know these Starpeople very well, I don't know their energies."

"I do," Tim said. "I know them. I think I could find them."

Aria shook her head. "But that means you would have

to leave here? Go back to the other side?"

Tim sighed. "Technically, I don't exist anyway, so no one would miss me. And I don't know if anyone else could do this. Besides, I have been here for twenty years feeling useless, it would be good to feel like I'm actually helping."

"I would miss you," Aria said, tears forming in her eyes. "I only just found you again."

Tim smiled at his favourite Faerie. "And we will see each other again. But this way, I get to see my Flame again too."

Aria sniffled and wiped away her unshed tears. "I know. I'll just miss you."

"Are you sure, Tim?" Velvet said. "This is a big ask."

Tim nodded. "It makes the most sense. After all, I know them. They will understand it all better coming from me."

Velvet smiled at the Starperson. "You really always were quite exceptional, Tim," she said. "Go to the Academy and find Bk and Laguz in the operations room. Tell them everything about the situation, and what you need to do. We will await a message from you to tell us what we need to do next."

"Got it, will do." He frowned. "What will you all do until then?"

Magenta sighed. "We will live our lives as normally as we can, and keep an eye out for any new developments that could tell us what Au is planning next."

"Ugh, normal life," Aria said grabbing a handful of crisps and crunching on them loudly while the others chuckled.

"Indeed," Magenta said wryly. "Do hurry, Tim, I have the same foreboding feeling as you. Au is cooking up something big, and I don't like it at all."

Tim nodded. "I will cross over tonight, and I will begin my mission."

"Oooh can we go to the movies together before you go?" Aria said, as she slurped her orange juice.

Tim chuckled and patted her knee. "I think that can be arranged. What do you want to see?"

"Armageddon?" Aria said innocently. The whole group erupted into laughter, and Aria laughed with them, but inside, her heart hurt.

# CHAPTER FIFTEEN

If anyone had asked her, Aria couldn't have told them what the movie was about. All she could remember was struggling to eat her popcorn while gripping tightly onto Tim's hand for two hours in the dark theatre, fighting back the tears that threatened, because she would soon have to say goodbye to him.

She wished they had more time together. She knew they would never have the same life as they'd had in the Diamond Age. That they wouldn't grow old together, still creating books and characters, travelling the world, and eating amazing food. Tim was already older than her in that reality, and in this one, he was another twenty years older. Even if he stayed, they wouldn't have nearly as long together.

She had a slight pang of guilt, as a character in the movie who looked like Linen appeared on the screen. But she knew her Flame would understand. She had told him everything when they had reunited, and he had encouraged her to come to Earth now, to help Tim. He knew that she had a big heart, and could love them both. And that she would return to him, just as soon as this mission was done.

But how would it end?

Aria and Tim walked out of the cinema, hand in hand, and for a few minutes, didn't speak. Aria was hyper-aware of his warm hand in hers, the cool breeze drying her unshed tears, and the scent of his subtle cologne. She was completely unaware of the cars streaming past, the other people walking by, the drizzle of rain hitting her face and the wail of sirens in the distance.

As far as she was concerned, it was just the two of them in the world.

"Did you enjoy it?" Tim asked, breaking the silence.

Aria glanced sideways at him. "Uh, yeah, it was good."

"You didn't really watch it, did you?" Tim said, smiling down at her.

She shook her head. He knew her too well. "How could you tell?"

"I could see the look in your eyes that you were in your own world, not in the one on the screen."

"You were watching me?" she asked, her cheeks reddening.

"I'd rather watch you than any movie," Tim said. "You are far more interesting."

Aria ducked her head and sighed. "I guess a movie was a silly idea. I should have asked you what you wanted to do. It's your last night on Earth, after all." Her voice cracked, and the tears she thought she had under control began to spill out.

Tim stopped walking and pulled her to the side, so they didn't disrupt the flow of pedestrians. He pulled her to him and crushed her in a bear hug. "I will see you again," he said softly in her ear. "I promise. This is not the end."

Aria nodded into his chest, not trusting herself to speak. It was taking all of her strength to not dissolve into a puddle of tears.

"Are you going to be okay?" Tim pulled back and looked at her.

Aria stared up at the alien, her tears still falling silently. She nodded again, even though she hated to lie. "Do you have to go now?" she whispered. "Or can we go to the park?"

Tim smiled. "Let's go to the park, then I will walk you home."

Aria frowned. "How are you planning to leave Earth?"

Tim sighed. "It's probably best you don't know. But I will do my best to leave no trace. Don't want any unnecessary search parties or wasted police work."

Aria frowned. "I will know you are gone. I will remember."

Tim nodded. "And that's why you should have these." He handed her his wallet and keys, and his watch. "I pay my rent in cash, and it's all paid up 'til the end of this month. Maybe you could clear out my things? You might need my research, but you can donate the rest. There's not much."

"So you definitely won't be coming back?" Aria asked, her heart heavy.

"I don't think I can. Au disabled the walk-in program. We were the last to be able to walk in."

Aria nodded and took his possessions and swallowed hard, past the lump that had formed in her throat. She placed them safely in her bag, and then took a deep breath.

"Let's go dance under the stars," she said.

"Yes, ma'am," Tim replied, taking her hand again as they set off down the street.

Long after Tim had walked her home, Aria sat at the kitchen table in the dark, turning his worn leather wallet over and over in her hands. Her heart ached as she tried not to think about how he was going to leave Earth, about how much she would miss him, after only having spent a few days with him again. After dancing barefoot on the cold damp grass in the park, they had collapsed in a breathless heap, and rolled onto their backs to look up at the stars. Much as he had in their previous life, Tim pointed out different constellations to her, and the more she looked, the more stars appeared.

It still amazed and awed her that these tiny little sparks of light, millions of miles away, were really the homes of Starpeople, just like Tim. She wondered how many Starpeople there were out there, living their lives, completely unaware of the other people and beings on other planets.

Aria sighed and opened his wallet, finding it devoid of anything except some cash and his fake ID.

She ran her finger over his tiny printed face and wished she had taken some photos of him on her phone. This tiny bit of plastic would be the only evidence that he had ever existed.

Other than the hole that was now in her heart, of course.

She closed her eyes and pictured his face as he stared up at the stars.

"Do you miss Zubenelgenubi?" she had whispered, shivering slightly as the damp of the grass seeped through her leggings. "Do you think you'll ever go back?"

He had reached his arm out and pulled her to his side, so that his warmth eased her shivers. He didn't respond for a while.

"I miss the light," he had replied. "It was like nothing else in the galaxy. It was bright, warm, but also just..." he sighed. "I can't even explain it. As for going back, if Au is right, there is no light there now, there is nothing to go back to. Even though," he waved his hand to the sky. "You can see it from here, clear and bright as ever. It takes so long for the light to reach us here, that we could be seeing the star as it was when I was still there, so long ago."

"I remember your light," Aria had said, recalling Tim in his Starperson form, when he had first arrived at the Academy. "You were beautiful."

Tim had chuckled. "You were the most curious thing I had ever seen, so tiny and green and fast, whizzing about here and there. Didn't quite know what to make of you, but I knew that I loved you."

Aria opened her eyes and looked down at Tim's face on his ID, shimmering in the moonlight coming through the window.

She remembered his eyes shining with unshed tears as he had stood at her door just a few hours before, trying to find the words to say goodbye. Finally, she had whispered, "Goodnight, Alien."

He had smiled and a lone tear fell, glinting in the streetlights. "Goodnight, Faerie."

But what she had really meant was, "I knew I loved you, too."

# STARLIGHT

## CHAPTER SIXTEEN

Once upon a time, a very, very, distant time, long ago, Starlight, the Angel of Destiny, had promised herself that she would never again set foot inside the Earth Angel Training Academy in the Fifth Dimension.

And yet here she was, again.

She sighed, annoyed with herself, but unable to stand by and watch any longer. She straightened up to her full height, flicked her long blonde hair that looked like strands of pure light over her shoulder, and entered the office of Brown Corduroy.

As the door appeared behind her, it seemed as though her entrance had gone unnoticed by the three who were deep in discussion, so she cleared her throat to get their attention.

If she had been in the mood, she might have laughed at their expressions. But at that moment, she hadn't a shred of humour left.

"Starlight!" Gold gasped, rising to his feet, while Corduroy's mouth simply dropped open, and Bk dropped his notebook.

"I never really enjoy saying this, but this time I must. I fucking told you so, didn't I?" Her voice rang out around the room, bouncing off the gleaming white walls of the small office.

Gold hung his head, and Bk gulped. Corduroy's mouth snapped shut and he looked like a scolded school boy.

The Angel of Destiny didn't often get angry, but when she did, it was something akin to a lightning show. She could feel the sparks of light shooting from her skin and hair, fizzing about her, likely creating a halo.

"Starlight, no one could have known that this was-"

"I knew," Starlight said, cutting Corduroy off with her sharp tone. "I knew that creating the time loop would create a complete disaster, and I told you that! Explicitly! And none of you listened. None of you," she said again, pointedly looking at her Flame who still refused to meet her gaze.

"How much do you know?" Bk asked timidly.

Starlight sighed and waved her hand to create a seat for her to sit down. She felt exhausted. But then, she always did in the Fifth Dimension. "I know everything, Bk, and I am very unimpressed. I mean, sending the Earth Angels back? To do what? Witness the destruction of the planet and everyone who lives on her? Why would you do that to them? Hasn't Velvet done enough? Suffered enough? You should have left everything well alone, let the planet rest. Then we wouldn't be having this issue right now, and I," she looked at Gold, "*we,* would be home, where we belong."

Gold sighed. "My dearest Starlight, you are of course right, and I regret not listening to you, in every moment. But, I must ask, if you knew, why did you wait? Why did you leave us in limbo for over twenty years? Why did you not stop the alien, Au?"

Starlight sighed and shook her head. "Because I wasn't watching you, or the Academy, or even Earth. I was working on a new project, and it took up all my focus."

Corduroy frowned. "So how do you know everything now?"

Starlight sighed. "Because I kept dreaming of Gold. And considering I do not dream, it was an unusual occurrence. Though I admit to ignoring it for some time. By the time I checked in, I found myself curious as to why he was visiting the Seventh Dimension, and so I decided to tune in and watch the most recent projections from Earth and the Academy. And quite frankly, I couldn't believe my eyes. And I have seen much in my vast existence."

No one dared meet her eye for a few moments, and Starlight felt some of her rage dissolve at the sight of her forlorn Flame, with nothing to say to defend himself. The problem was, she knew that he'd had good intentions. They all had.

But she also knew what they said about the road paved with good intentions. And what had been created on Earth at that current moment was indeed hellish.

"What should we do?" Gold asked, finally lifting his head and looking at her.

She closed her eyes and shook her head. "I have run the projections forwards, backwards and sideways, and I'm afraid all we can do is ride it out. I cannot see a path through this that will leave the planet in a good state."

Starlight could see that it was not what Gold had hoped to hear. And she felt a flicker of annoyance at being the one to cause disappointment, when he was the one who had caused the mess in the first place.

At least he seemed to have glossed over the fact that she had ignored his calls for more than two decades, and not come to his aid. She was sure he would have something to say about it later though.

"I can't just ride it out," Bk said, his voice still shaking slightly. "I will keep trying to sort out the mess that Au created of the machine, and keep running potential scenarios through the system."

Starlight raised an eyebrow. "You think your technology is more advanced than me? You think that it can come up with something that I have not?" She tried not to sound incredulous, but she failed.

Bk shrugged. "Probably not. But it is the same technology that Au has used to create the chaos, so perhaps it holds the answers to ending it. And I can't just sit around and wait. I will keep working on it, even if you have already given up." He picked up his notebook from where it still lay on the floor, straightened his clothes and then nodded at them. "I'll report back if I find anything."

Corduroy nodded back and Gold muttered a thank you. Bk exited hastily. For all his bravado, he seemed very pleased to get away from the angry Angel of Destiny.

There was an awkward silence after he left.

Finally Starlight looked at Gold and found him staring at her curiously.

"You haven't given up, have you?" It sounded more like a statement than a question, but there was doubt in his eyes.

"You can still read me, after all this time," she replied wearily, rubbing her eyes. "I am still running projections, but there are so many variables, none of the paths are a certainty, they depend on many, many people making the right choices. And as we know, humans, or even Earth

Angels, are not the most reliable in making the right decisions."

Gold sighed. "No, I know this more than most. But," he looked at her hopefully. "There is a glimmer of a possibility that we can turn this situation around? That it's not too late?"

Starlight churlishly didn't want to give him the hope that he desperately sought, she didn't feel like he deserved it. But she never could resist making her Flame smile.

"There is a glimmer," she said, her heart lifting when his face creased into a smile.

* * *

"I thought I might find you here."

Starlight looked away from the projection in front of her and saw her Flame standing by the entrance to the Atlantis Garden. She waved away the projection which dissolved into tiny glittering lights and patted the empty seat next to her on the golden bench.

Gold approached cautiously and sat next to her, but not close enough so that they touched. She knew he could still feel the hostility in her energy.

It was getting harder to stay angry with him the longer she spent in his presence. In truth, she had only stayed angry with him for this long because she hadn't gone anywhere near him. Now, seeing his face, with his twitching eye, and his beautiful smile, smelling his scent and hearing his voice, her resolve to remain angry dissolved just as her projections just had.

As if sensing the shift in her, Gold asked softly.

"Why didn't you come when I called you? Did you

really hate me that much, that you could ignore me?"

Starlight sighed. "I was finally moving on with my own work when I first heard your call. I was happy. And then, out of nowhere, you were in my mind. In my thoughts, all the time. And it was infuriating. Because yes, I was angry. I had told you not to create the loop. Not to give in to the desires of the humans. They'd had their time, they were done. And they'd had the best possible lives they were going to have. I mean, the Diamond Age! How could they possibly improve upon that?" Starlight stood up and began pacing back and forth on the jewel-strewn path, feeling agitated again. "But oh no, you wanted to give them the chance to do it over and over again. Because what harm could it do?" she scoffed. "And now we have this ridiculous mess on our hands. So yes, I was angry, and I wanted nothing to do with it. I told you my views, and I asked you, I *begged* you to come home with me. To be in the stars. And you refused. So yes, I ignored your calls. I blocked out your voice. And honestly, I think being trapped in that single moment all those years was your penance for taking part in such a terrible idea."

Gold sighed. "All that may be true," he said, his ancient voice exhausted. "But was that not penance enough? I am trying my best to fix it, and once I was released from that moment, I stopped calling, did I not? I didn't expect you to come and sort out my mess."

Starlight stopped pacing and looked at him. "You did. But when I didn't hear your voice or dream of you for a while, I got worried. Because then I thought something really awful must have happened, and that's when I tuned in, only to find all of this."

Gold tried to smile. "So you do still care about me?

Enough to finally check?"

Starlight shook her head and his smile disappeared. "Gold, despite my best efforts to eradicate you from my existence, I will never, ever not love you, care about you, and want the best for you. But that also makes me really quite angry."

Gold stood up and walked over to where she stood by the marble statues of Velvet and Laguz. He opened his arms and wrapped them around her, pulling her tightly to him. She tried to resist, her body stiff and unyielding.

But it didn't take long for her to soften, for her face to press against the golden damask of his robes, for her arms to encircle his.

"I love you more than the moon and the stars," he whispered.

"I love you more than my own sanity, apparently," she muttered back.

His chest rumbled with laughter against her ear, and before she could stop herself, Starlight smiled for the first time in a very long while.

# CHAPTER SEVENTEEN

"Do you really think that Velvet and the others can change things? It took a huge number of Earth Angels last time, not to mention the star downloads. A small group of Awakened Earth Angels is like a tiny drop in the ocean, surely?"

Gold and Starlight had walked around the gardens at the Academy several times, discussing potential outcomes and ideas, and they were now sat in the Angelic Garden, in front of the waterfall.

Gold considered her question for a few moments. "Do you doubt your sister's ability to make a difference?"

"Of course not," Starlight answered immediately. "But she is up against a mighty force. Not to mention is over twenty years behind. It's a big ask."

Gold nodded. "You're right. It is. Would her odds be greater if we got her more help?"

Starlight frowned. "How? Seek out all the Earth Angels scattered about the dimensions and galaxies, gather them up and make them conscious?"

"Yes. Why not?"

Starlight watched the water hitting the smooth rocks

in the pool of crystal clear water before them and thought about the possibilities of sending an army of Earth Angels to assist Velvet. Deciding it wouldn't hurt to do a proper check, she ran a projection of the idea, which appeared before them both in the air, and ran forwards from the present moment at a speed that a human could never have comprehended. But neither of them were human, so they understood it perfectly.

"It improves things somewhat?" Gold said hesitatingly. He hadn't seen all of the projections that Starlight had, so it was difficult for him to compare.

"Yes, slightly. There is still so much that will not change. And the world will still end in darkness, just not quite so quickly. I think our blindspot is not knowing what Au is planning next. If we knew that, perhaps we can come up with a better solution."

"Indeed. And I know that Bk is working tirelessly to find out what her plans are. He feels terrible that his machine was sabotaged in this way."

"The machine should never had been given the capabilities it has. You cannot trust machines. They have no feelings, no morality." Starlight rubbed her eyes tiredly. The Fifth Dimension really did exhaust her.

"Neither do some men," Gold said wryly, making Starlight chuckle.

"True. But with men, there is the possibility of learning some empathy. Of them doing the right thing. Machines simply do what they are programmed to do, whether it is right or wrong. They have nothing to lose."

Gold reached out to touch her hand, and Starlight pulled away, shifting over on the bench out of reach. Gold sighed. "Do you think you will ever forgive me?" he asked.

"For doing the wrong thing? Even though you are not a machine, but an Elder, an Old Soul who should know better?" Starlight shook her head. "I don't know. You know that I love you, you know that I want nothing more to be in your embrace, that I have missed you desperately. But you also made choices that I cannot condone. And now Earth is in peril, the Earth Angels have been called out of retirement into action again, and all because an old man just couldn't give up playing god."

Gold winced and rested his hand back in his lap.

Starlight hated being so blunt, so harsh with her Flame, but she knew that if she gave in too easily, and let him off too quickly, they would be no doubt having another similar conversation another few eons down the line. He had to understand how catastrophic his actions had been. And how she might not be able to help him to fix it. That this time, it may well all end in darkness, and when that happened, it would be on him.

"I was selfish," Gold admitted. "I wanted to give humans the chance to keep going, to keep experiencing their lives, to let them make different choices, to spend time in physicality with their loved ones. But my vision was short-sighted. I did not consider the long-term ramifications. And of course I had no idea that this current situation was a possibility."

Starlight didn't respond. Her resolve was wavering, and she didn't trust herself to speak.

"I won't trivialise the situation with trying to apologise for my actions. I know that you warned us, you warned me, and that I didn't listen, and my selfishness and stubbornness pushed you away. I know I should have listened, and I should have allowed the Earth to rest, and come with you to the stars."

"So why didn't you?" Starlight whispered, tears forming in her eyes.

Gold was quiet for a few moments, and the sound of the waterfall seemed amplified as Starlight waited for his reply and did her best not to allow the tears to fall.

"Because I couldn't let it go."

Starlight frowned and looked at her Flame. "Let what go?"

"My purpose. Standing on the edge of the mists, waiting for humans to arrive so that I could ask them the ultimate question, has been my main and pretty much only function for my entire existence. And I couldn't let it go. What would I have done in the stars? What would my purpose have been? Who would I have been?" Gold looked down at his lap, he appeared to be ashamed by his admission, and Starlight could feel his shame and his disgust with himself.

She shifted closer to him on the bench and reached over to take his hand, then looked at him and waited for him to look at her.

"We would have figured that out together. The universe is vast, and I have no doubt that you would have found a new purpose. You would have flourished in the stars with me. Why didn't you tell me of your worries? We could have avoided all of this if I had known of your fears."

Gold gripped her hand tightly. "I'm sorry. I should have. I was a fool to think that I could just keep going, just keep doing what I have always done, and hope that it might last forever. I was afraid of the unknown."

Starlight chuckled. "If the humans only knew just how very human you are, they would see you in a whole different light."

Gold smiled. "I guess I have spent so much time with

them, I may as well be a human." He frowned. "Did you hear that?"

Starlight listened carefully and heard the sound of windchimes. "Bk?" she guessed. "Maybe he has some news."

Gold stood up and pulled Starlight to her feet. "Let's go and see."

Starlight smiled at his renewed enthusiasm, and hand in hand, they headed back into the Academy.

*　*　*

Gold and Starlight entered the operations room to find a flurry of activity. Bk and Dhalia were shouting instructions at each other, and dancing around each other, pressing buttons and turning dials, and there was a veritable light show of symbols and lines across the many screens in front of them.

"You called?" Gold said curiously.

Bk paused and looked up at them and grinned. "Yes, sorry, would have called properly but as you can see, it's all systems go."

"Yes we can see that, what's going on?" Starlight asked, feeling slightly irritated and impatient.

"I'm here!" Corduroy announced as he arrived, Laguz hot on his heels. "What's going on?"

"We've done it!" Dahlia squealed.

"Done what?" Starlight demanded, her hopes lifting. "You've undone the damage that Au has done to the machine?"

"Oh, er, no," Dahlia said, looking a little deflated. "We've got the walk-in program fixed. We should now be able to send Earth Angels to Earth into other bodies. And we can even just send them in their own bodies. We don't have to rely on waking up those who were there during this age."

"So I can join Velvet and the others?" Laguz asked.

"Yes," Bk said. "You could walk into Greg's body again, with his spirit's permission of course, or you could go as you are. We still have some work to do, but it should be ready pretty soon."

"Looks like we can send that extra help," Starlight murmured to Gold.

"Should we send word out to the other realms and dimensions? I am sure there are more who might like to return to help," Corduroy asked. "Velvet said that Emerald and Mica were keen, and that they may be able to find more."

"Yes, that would be a good plan," Bk said, still rushing about, setting dials to certain settings, and studying the symbols on the screen.

Starlight stared at the screens, trying to make sense of it, but the technology of the Zubenelgenubians was beyond even her comprehension. "Good work, you two. Are you getting anywhere with working out what Au has planned next? Or how we can find her?" Starlight still felt on edge, being in the dark as to the plans of the rogue alien.

Bk shook his head. "I'm still running the possibilities, it feels like she is planning something that has never been done before, and as such, the machine doesn't have past precedent to help it predict what she is about to do."

Starlight sighed. "What about you?"

Bk frowned. "Me?"

"What would you do? If you were Au? How would you cause the most harm, the most suffering, the most chaos?"

Bk's eyebrows raised. "I am not Au. I wouldn't want to do that. We Zubenelgenubians are light beings by nature. Au is very much the exception."

Starlight shook her head. "Nevermind. I just thought perhaps you might have some insight into how her mind might work."

"I'm sorry, Starlight. But I have not experienced the darkness that Au has, not even in my stint as a human on Earth. She was alone on a dying planet for aeons. The darkness that must have grown in her is unlike anything I can comprehend."

Starlight nodded. "I understand. Well, we had better leave you to it. Corduroy, get word to Emerald and Mica. Laguz, perhaps you can visit the Seventh and some other dimensions to see if there are any Earth Angels who might be willing to help. Gold," she said, turning to her Flame. "You must visit the Angelic Realm and see if there are Angels who will join the mission."

"What will you do?" the Elder inquired.

"I will visit the Children. We have asked far too much of them already, but I will visit the Indigos, Crystals, Rainbows and Diamonds and see if they would help us this one last time. I cannot promise anything, but if they can arrive in their own forms, it might just work."

"Isn't it going to be slightly crazy, sending hundreds, maybe thousands of Earth Angels to Earth en masse?" Laguz asked. "How will they live? The ones in their own bodies will have no identities, no homes, no money."

"We can spread them out across the planet, so there isn't a huge wave arriving in one spot, that's possible, right Bk?" Starlight said.

Bk nodded distractedly while he was busy doing

something on the control panel.

"And I am sure that the Earth Angels already there will help them. It just feels like the only way to change the course of action that Au has set in motion is to hit Earth with a huge amount of light, and in this scenario, the light is us."

"Us?" Gold asked. "You are going too?"

"No," Starlight said. "This is not my mission, not my mess. I will remain here. But you will go."

Gold gulped but nodded. "Of course."

Starlight clapped her hands, making Dahlia jump. "There's no time to waste, we must set the plan in motion. Bk, let us know when it is ready to go, we will gather whoever we can to the main hall."

Bk nodded. "Will do."

Out in the hallway, Corduroy went to his office, and Laguz set off towards the gardens. Gold turned to Starlight. "I will see you back here soon?"

Starlight nodded. "I will be as quick as I can. I will not force the Children to come, it will be entirely of their own free will."

Gold nodded. "I feel much guilt that they are to be asked at all. That anyone should be. Though I do wish you were to come too."

"Your guilt is not helpful here," Starlight replied, ignoring his attempt to guilt her into going with him. "Go to the Angels, and see who you can gather. Now is the time for action, not regret." Starlight leaned over to kiss her Flame on the cheek. "Good luck."

"You too, my love."

# CHAPTER EIGHTEEN

The Golden City of the Indigo planet glowed brightly in the darkness, making Starlight feel a wave of déjà vu as she stood at the edge of the city, gathering her energy and courage to enter the gate and once again, ask for too much.

With one last deep breath, Starlight reached out to touch the gate, asking permission to enter the city, and the gate gracefully swung away to admit her. She walked up the golden path to the main castle where she knew she would find her dear old friend.

"Starlight." The whisper of her name reached her a moment before the orb of golden light at the doors of the castle transformed into a beautiful Child.

"Indigo," Starlight said with a smile. "I have missed you."

"You have not visited in many eons, I would like to say it is good to see you, but I can see from your aura that perhaps you do not come with good tidings."

Starlight sighed. I'm afraid I do not. And I'm afraid I have come to ask too much of you all once again."

The Child looked disappointed. "We have lived in

harmony and love ever since we left Earth after the Diamond Age. All of our lost siblings also came home, we have been whole and happy and doing our best to be a bright light in the universe. I do not think we wish to do anything else."

Starlight nodded. "I understand. It was wrong of me to come, to even dream of asking. You have done more than enough for me, and for the humans on Earth. I'm sorry to have bothered you."

Her heart heavy, Starlight turned away from the Indigo Child and started heading down the path.

"Wait."

Starlight stopped and her heart lifted slightly. She turned to look at the Child.

"Ask me anyway. I cannot promise the answer you wish for. But you have come all this way. I can at least listen to your request."

Starlight smiled. "Thank you. I will try to explain as best I can, I don't even understand all of the technology involved, but I will do my best."

The Child walked over to a bench overlooking the city, where her siblings in orb form were zipping about, unaware of the potentially universe-shattering conversation that was about to take place.

Starlight joined the Child on the bench and cleared her throat. "I'm not sure where to begin," she admitted.

"Begin at the end," the Child said softly.

* * *

By the time Starlight had repeated the tale of the current chaos on Earth for the third time, she was wearier than she had ever felt in her entire existence.

The Rainbows had been far more accepting and calm than the Indigos and Crystals, and were quicker to agree to go back to Earth. Though they had finally agreed, Starlight was still unsure as to whether the Indigos and Crystals would indeed go to the Academy. And she wouldn't blame them at all if they didn't. Their worlds were stunning. There was no hunger, war, violence, hate, or fear. Who would leave that glorious light to assist a race that didn't even want to help themselves?

Starlight looked at the Diamond Child. "I will not in any way expect you to come. The choice is yours. I feel awful for even asking. You brought about the greatest age the Earth and humans have ever seen, you have done your part."

"And yet, that reality no longer exists? What we created was simply, overwritten?" the Diamond Child asked sadly.

Starlight sighed. "Yes. It exists now only in the memories of the Earth Angels who experienced it. Earth is now heading for an entirely different future, and much darker ending to the age of humans."

The Diamond Child's light visibly dimmed, her aura grew darker, and Starlight's heart hurt at the thought of such beautiful souls experiencing the state of chaos that the Earth was currently in.

"Say no," Starlight whispered. "There is no expectation here. This battle is not yours."

"The Rainbows, Indigos and Crystals are returning?" the Diamond Child asked.

Starlight nodded. "They have agreed to come, but I have made it clear that there will be no judgement nor consequences should they change their minds. I am hoping that they don't come. I didn't want to ask them to in the first place."

"I appreciate your love and concern for us, but we will come. We cannot allow our brothers and sisters to go alone. We will come to the Academy, ready to return to Earth to do whatever we can to help."

Starlight closed her eyes and bowed her head. "You are far more forgiving and beautiful than I," she whispered.

"You shall not be coming with us?" the Diamond Child asked, correctly reading her meaning.

Starlight shook her head. "I cannot forgive my Flame for what he has done. For creating this chaos, this darkness, that my sister must sort out, and that is forcing me to be here, asking too much of you." She sighed. "I shall return to my home in the stars, and I shall not be checking in to see how it all turns out. I cannot bear to watch."

The Diamond Child smiled sadly. "Maybe one day, you will find it possible to forgive. But I understand. You must do what you need to do to protect yourself. You have been in service for a very long time. You deserve a time of peace."

Starlight smiled back. "I appreciate you giving up your peace, but truly, if you do not come, it will be okay with me."

"Thank you, Angel of Destiny. I shall confer with my kin, but I expect I will be seeing you again very soon."

Starlight stood up from the glittering chair and nodded. "Be the light."

"Be the light," the Child echoed.

* * *

Starlight couldn't bring herself to return immediately to the operations room upon her return to the Academy. Instead, she wandered the gardens for a while, trying to forgive herself for having asked such beautiful light beings to enter the fray, despite the damage it might do to them.

When she felt she could hide no longer, she walked slowly towards the offices, and entered the operations room to find it in a frenzied state of activity.

She scanned the room, noting that her Flame wasn't there, but she saw a soul who had not been there when she left. A soul whom she was most glad to see in that moment. Her hope that they might succeed in this crazy mission rallied.

"Tm!" She stepped towards the Starperson and engulfed him in a hug. He took a moment to respond in kind, as he appeared to be shocked by her greeting.

"Starlight," he said as she stepped back. "I must say, I hadn't expected such warm greetings upon my return. Perhaps I should have come back sooner."

Starlight chuckled. "Seeing you has lifted my spirits. I do hope you bring good news?"

Tm, tilted his head to one side, and Starlight's heart sank a little.

"Aria, Velvet and the others found me, and I shared my findings with them. We decided that it made the most sense for me to find the souls involved in these realms, and to convince them to return to their bodies, to help us turn this situation around. It seemed an impossible task to get near them on Earth, and besides, most would be unconscious. I thought if I could explain to them, and then they return consciously, it would help."

"And Au? Was she with you?"

Tm shook his head. "No, we parted ways early on, and I have no idea what guise she is under now. But I have been tracking all the changes, and I can tell that she has something big planned, I just haven't quite worked out what it is yet."

Starlight sighed. Though not terrible news, it still wasn't quite what she was hoping for. "That is the feeling we have too, though my projections are not capable of predicting it, and neither are Bk's machines, it seems."

Bk looked up at the mention of his name, then looked away, his expression sad.

"Whatever it is, I am hoping I can find my kin and convince them to abort their plans. They likely have no idea what their replica on Earth is doing, if they are in other realms."

"You would have thought word might have got to them by now," Starlight said thoughtfully. "We have been spreading the word far and wide throughout the galaxy for Earth Angels to come back here and go to Earth to help."

Tm shrugged. "Maybe, but knowing them, they are somewhere wrapped up in their own worlds. I will go and seek them out, and see what I can do."

"He is taking Au's ship," Bk said. "I have upgraded it slightly, so that he can travel to other realms as well as the far reaches of this galaxy and beyond."

Starlight nodded. "When do you leave?"

"I will go today, I was just giving Bk and Laguz all of the information I have on the situation. In case it was of any use."

"I'm sure it will be. It was thanks to the recording you left behind that we had any idea at all what was going on," Bk said. "Thank you. I know you risked being caught by Au."

Tm nodded. "I still cannot quite believe that she has

done all of this. It seems inconceivable that a being of light could create such darkness."

"To be fair," Laguz spoke up from the hidden room. "All she did was tip the scales towards darkness. The humans did the rest all by themselves. And without the Earth Angels being there consciously, there was nothing to balance the scales."

Tm sighed. "Still, I tried to appeal to her light, to her inner spark, but it seemed to have gone entirely. I fear that perhaps we won't be able to reverse the damage she has done, or to improve it in any way."

Starlight reached out to touch Tm's arm. "We will just do our best, and see what happens. At this point, none of us know what will happen. But in time, when we look back, we will all know that we did our best, and that we did what we could. That is all any of us can do."

Tm sighed. "Thank you. I will do my best, I have been waiting more than twenty years to be of some use. I promise I will not let you down."

Starlight shook her head. "It is impossible. You cannot let me, or anyone else down, because you have already done far more than any of us could possibly ask for."

This time, it was Starlight who was surprised when Tm engulfed her in a hug.

"Be the light," Starlight whispered.

"Be the light," Tm replied. He let her go, and then with one final check with Bk on the status of the flying craft, he left the operations room, and set off on his mission.

Starlight watched him leave through the disappearing door, silently wishing him good luck, and hoping, despite what she had said, that he wouldn't let them down. When the door reappeared she turned back to Bk.

"Now what?" she asked.

"Now we wait," Bk replied.

# CHAPTER NINETEEN

The main hall at the Academy had never been so big, or so full of apprehension and excitement. Starlight stood on the stage next to Gold, as they awaited instructions from Bk on sending the vast roomful of galactic beings back to Earth. Her heart hurt as she looked around and saw all the Children. They had all come, every last one. There was to be more Golden Age Children on Earth at one time then there had ever been. So if that didn't help to turn things around, she didn't know what would.

Corduroy was pacing back and forth, clearly agitated and irritated. He was annoyed that Starlight had insisted he and Athena both stay at the Academy, and not join the others on Earth. But Emerald and Mica had advised that it was best that the Goddess of War and the Professor of Death stay on the Other Side, to give Earth a better chance of reviving. Starlight knew that Corduroy was desperate to get revenge against the rogue alien, and so she agreed with the Angels. More revenge was not what was needed on Earth at that time.

"Where's Laguz?" she asked her Flame quietly. She was

surprised to not see him in the room, he had also been desperate to get to Earth, and she saw no reason why he shouldn't join his Flame.

"He's not going," Gold said, not meeting her gaze.

Starlight frowned. "What? Why not? Surely Velvet could use his assistance?"

Gold closed his eyes, but it did not stop the twitch. "I asked him to remain, for now. He will join us at a later date."

Starlight could tell he had no intention of explaining further. So she would simply find Laguz after everyone had left and ask him herself.

She sighed. "What is taking so long? I thought Bk said they were nearly ready?"

Gold shrugged. "Perhaps there has been a hiccup."

As though he had heard her, Starlight heard Bk's voice in her ear. "Um, Starlight? Could you come to the operations room, please? We need your assistance?"

Starlight rolled her eyes. "It would appear that there has indeed been a hiccup. Coming?" She held her hand out to her Flame, who grasped it firmly.

"Corduroy?" she called out softly to the pacing Old Soul.

Corduroy stopped mid-pace and spun to face her. "Is it time?"

She shook her head slightly. "Bk needs us for a moment, hold the fort?" She nodded her head at the large buzzing crowd.

Corduroy frowned but nodded back.

Starlight squeezed Gold's hand gently, and they disappeared from the stage, leaving only a sprinkle of gold lights behind.

∗   ∗   ∗

"What is it?" Starlight asked the moment they reappeared in the operations room. Her heart sank when she saw the stricken expression on the face of the small pink Faerie at the control panel.

Bk came into the room from the hidden room where the machine was whirring away. Starlight could see Laguz sat at the machine, his head in his hands.

"We have hit a stumbling block," Bk said.

"How bad?" Gold asked wearily. Though Starlight detected a faint hint of relief in his tone.

Bk sighed and looked at Dahlia, who shrugged her tiny shoulders. He looked back at Starlight. "The only way to reactivate the walk-in program, and to send all of the souls currently waiting in the main hall to Earth, is to reboot the internet."

Starlight raised her eyebrows. "That's it? You knew that a few days ago, what's the problem?"

Bk winced. "Well it's not a simple restart. I was hoping to find a way to limit the damage, and the amount of time it would be down, but it seems that rebooting will likely wipe the internet clean. And it will be down for several days."

"Clean? As in, all the data on the internet will be gone?" Gold asked.

Bk nodded. "Yes, anything not stored in local servers or on people's devices will be gone. Fifty years of stuff, gone. A clean slate. No social media, no websites, no online commerce."

Starlight didn't know what to say. They needed the walk-ins, the Earth needed their light. But the world at the current time relied entirely on the internet. Would wiping it clean help or hinder their efforts to save the humans from impending doom?

"What about banking? Communications?" Gold asked, his face looking decidedly grey.

"There's no way to know for certain," Dahlia said, "But the likelihood will be that it will all be gone. All depends on what is stored on servers. And at the very least, it will be completely down for several days, which could cause mass panic."

"What about restoring the internet to a previous version after the reboot?" Laguz asked, coming out of the hidden room to join them.

Bk frowned and looked at Dahlia. "That's possible, I guess. I can do a backup now, on the machine, and then try to restore it. But the world will still be without the internet while we reboot, and will likely believe that it is all gone, before I can try to restore it."

Starlight turned to an empty wall and started running through projections. But as before, the unknowns of the technology she didn't understand limited her capability to predict the most likely outcome.

After a few moments she waved the projections away and turned back to the others. They all seemed to be awaiting her final word. Of course. Then it could be her fault when things went horribly wrong.

"Do it. Back it up. Reboot the internet, get the walk-ins to Earth, and then try to restore." She could hardly believe the words she was saying, she was no tech geek by any means. "We will just deal with the fallout afterward. Who knows? Perhaps if the humans cannot use the internet to communicate for a short while, they might actually remember how to speak to people in person. Hell, they might even meet their own neighbours, or write a letter!"

Bk didn't look convinced, Laguz looked apprehensive, and Gold was the colour of ash. But all three men nodded, and Bk and Laguz returned to the machine, while Dahlia fluttered about at the control panel.

"We shall return to the main hall. We shall brief the group as a whole, and then await your signal. Do you anticipate it taking long?" Starlight asked

"Honestly? It may be a while. And I can only send you all once the system has rebooted." Bk called out from the hidden room.

"We shall do our best to entertain everyone," Gold said. "But please do work as quickly as possible."

Starlight reached her hand out to Gold, knowing that it would likely be the last time she ever touched her Flame. She gripped his hand tightly. His eyes met hers, and he nodded. He knew too. She closed her eyes and turned them both into glittering lights.

# Velvet

## CHAPTER TWENTY

It was a week after Tim had left, and Velvet and the other Earth Angels had resumed their lives. Human life seemed so alien to them, that they mostly just spent their time messaging each other in a group chat, discussing possible ways to change things on Earth. They all knew they just had to wait. To be patient.

But patience was a virtue that Velvet felt she had very little of.

Bored with herself, and feeling restless in her small flat, which was a far cry from her beautiful ocean home in the Seventh Dimension, Velvet flopped in front of her small TV and flicked through the channels. She needed an escape, and when she found an old favourite, she set down the remote and allowed herself to get wrapped up in the fantasy.

When it reached the scene that always gave her the chills, Velvet felt a shiver through her body when Gandalf uttered the words:

"Look to my coming on the first light of the fifth day. At dawn, look to the East."

The lights in the room flickered, and then the image on the TV froze. Velvet shivered and got up to grab a jumper. She slipped it on, then picked up the remote. She tried to refresh the movie, but nothing was working. Frowning, she picked up her phone, and saw that there was no signal, no internet. She went to her router, and saw that the light was off, indicating no signal.

She tutted. "Typical." She had a look on her phone to see if a neighbour's Wi-Fi was listed, perhaps if they still had signal she could connect to it. But there were no networks listed. She had hoped to message Aria, so she slipped her shoes on, grabbed her coat, and decided to head to a café in town. She could at least get a nice cake and drink, which might alleviate her boredom somewhat. It felt so frustrating to be on Earth, just waiting to find out what to do next. She wished they had figured out a better way of communicating with those in the Fifth Dimension. She hated feeling out of the loop.

She slammed the door behind her and went down the hallway, down the stairwell and out of the main door into the street. As she walked the short distance to the high street, she noticed that people were behaving a bit strangely, but she couldn't work out why that was. By the time she arrived at the café, she realised that she hadn't seen a single person on their phone, when normally, the streets were full of people staring down at the small device in their hands.

She got into the café and sighed when she saw a sign at the counter saying their Wi-Fi was down.

Was that it? Was the signal down everywhere for everyone?

She took her phone out and woke the screen up. There was still nothing.

"Seems like the whole network is down," the woman in line behind her commented. "Are you ordering?"

"Oh," Velvet looked up to see that she was at the front of the line. "Yes, sorry." She chose a cake and ordered a latte, figuring she may as well at least get something tasty to make up for the wasted trip. She turned to the lady behind her. "Any ideas when it will be back up?"

The woman shook her head. "No idea. But pretty much everything is down, including payment systems." She pointed to the rest of the text on the sign, which said cash only.

Velvet winced. "Shit, I don't have any cash." She waved to the barista who was already making her order. "I'm sorry, I don't have any cash. I didn't see that bit of the sign."

"Don't worry," the woman next to her in the line said. "I've got this." She ordered herself a coffee and a slice of banana bread and handed the barista the cash.

"Are you sure?" Velvet asked, genuinely touched that a complete stranger would buy her food.

The woman smiled. "Sure, enjoy. I hope you've brought a book? I don't think the internet will be back for a bit."

Velvet smiled back. "Thank you, really. And yeah, I do have a few on my Book app, will have a read." She moved to the end of the counter, picked up her order and smiled in thanks at the woman again before sitting down by the window of the café. She sipped her latte for a few moments before picking up her phone and finding a book to read. Luckily, she had downloaded a few the day before, so she tapped on the first one and swiped to the first page.

She started nibbling on her cake, but soon forgot it was there as she lost herself in the fictional drama on the page, forgetting her own for the moment.

Velvet stared at the newspaper in disbelief, having been reduced to buying a copy after two days of no internet and no access to TV or radio broadcasts.

The headline took up the entire front page.

INTERNET ARMAGEDDON?

She scanned the article, it seemed that there was no idea when the internet might return, what had caused it to shut down, and everything had come to a screaming halt, globally. No one could take payments, the stock markets were in chaos, communications had been reduced to old school letters and landline calls, of which most people didn't have anymore because everything had been switched to digital.

Even the newspaper itself had struggled to produce the paper due to lack of internet.

Velvet frowned. The fact that no one knew the source of the issue was making her wonder. Was Au behind this? Was this part of her plan to bring the world to its knees so that she could take over? Had she shut down the internet to take control of the planet?

For the millionth time she checked her phone only to see that there was no connection. Why on Earth had she and the other Earth Angels not exchanged addresses? At least she'd managed to find some cash in the flat, getting money out was almost impossible seeing as the banks were barely functioning. People weren't panicking too badly yet, but Velvet felt like they were on the edge of mass panic.

She folded the paper up and tucked it into her bag, then without thinking too much about it, found herself heading to the bus stop to get the bus to the park where they'd all met for the picnic after they'd arrived back.

For some reason, she had a gut feeling that the others might do the same.

Forty-five minutes later, Velvet stepped off the bus and made her way towards the park. Having read the newspaper in more detail, she was feeling even more disturbed by the current events and was even more convinced that the rogue alien was behind it all. What other explanation was there?

She reached the edge of the park and scanned the area as she entered, hoping that she would see a familiar face. As she approached a bench near where they had picnicked, she saw the back of a familiar blonde head.

"Aria?" she called out as she got closer, hoping it was her Faerie friend and not a random stranger.

The blonde spun around, and Velvet saw the relief on the Faerie's face.

"Oh, Velvet, thank the goddess!" She jumped up and ran over to the Old Soul, throwing her arms around her.

Velvet hugged her back, relief also flooding her body. "I had hoped you might be here, I had no way of contacting you, or the others!"

"I've been going crazy," Aria said, pulling away. They went back to the bench and sat down. "I've been sat here all day just hoping someone might come. What is going on? Is it Au? Has she taken over? Is this the end? I thought we had more time. Tm won't have had enough time to find everyone yet."

Velvet shook her head. "I have no idea, it feels like it might be down to Au. Maybe this was the big thing she had planned? To bring the whole world to its knees? It's kind of crazy just how much is dependent on an internet connection."

Aria sighed. "This is why the alien tech was a bad idea, and why things were so much better in our Diamond Age reality, when the Starpeople scaled their tech back. In that reality we never lost communication with each other, because we weren't completely reliant on the net. This is a disaster!"

"It is," Velvet agreed. "It hadn't even occurred to me to ensure we would have other methods to communicate other than through message apps. How will we reach the others? How will we know what to do?"

Aria was quiet for a while. "We found each other, perhaps we could try calling them, energetically?"

Velvet shrugged. "Can't hurt. Let's try it."

They both sat back on the bench and closed their eyes. To any passers-by they appeared to be just enjoying the sunshine, but the women were concentrating hard on calling out through the ether to their friends, in the hopes they would hear them and come to them.

"I wish we knew that Tim made it, and what Bk is doing," Aria said after a few moments. "You would think they could find a way to communicate, even without the net."

Velvet opened her eyes and frowned. "I have been thinking the same thing. What if they have though? And we haven't realised?"

"How? I haven't noticed any messages."

Something was tugging at the periphery of Velvet's mind. "Gandalf," she muttered. "Gold. Gold is coming."

Aria's eyebrows shot up. "He is? How do you know?"

"Look to my coming on the fifth day. At dawn, look to the east," Velvet recited. She knew the words to the movie trilogy by heart. "I think it will be here, that the internet and mobile signal will be down for five days, and then Gold will arrive. Hopefully, with the others." Velvet felt her heart lift. What if Laguz was with him? Surely he would be. She sighed. "I could be completely wrong and the internet crashing at that exact moment in the movie was a pure fluke."

"Let's assume you're right, what's the plan?"

Velvet thought for a few moments. "We need to find a way to contact the others. Let's go through our messages and look for clues of their whereabouts, but also just keep calling them here. Are you able to be here every day? You're close by, right?"

Aria nodded. "Yes, I can be here every day, I haven't got anything else to do. I will stick to this bench, and hope that they hear us and come here. Then what?"

"Once we've made contact, we can tell them to be here at dawn, on the fifth day from the shutdown, which will be Thursday. Wait! Thursday is Summer Solstice. Huh, that's quite the timing."

"That definitely feels like a sign," Aria agreed.

Velvet lifted her shoulders. "Let's hope that we're right, and that Gold and the others will arrive, and they will know what to do." A thought occurred to her then, and she frowned.

"What is it?" Aria asked, perceptive to her shifts in mood as always.

"What if this hasn't all been caused by Au? If the message was from Gold, and they knew the internet would be down for five days, then what if this is them? Bk and Laguz and Corduroy? In which case, perhaps shutting it down was the only way to stop Au's big plan?"

Aria's eyebrows shot up. "Wow, yeah, I mean, that

would make sense, but wow, it's a huge thing to do, causing worldwide chaos in order to prevent worldwide chaos."

Velvet chuckled. "It does seem a little mad, and makes me wonder what on Earth Au's plan was."

"Aliens are super smart, it was probably something that none of us could even imagine."

"I think you're right," Velvet said. "The Starpeople always have a way of surprising me."

"And causing headaches," Aria giggled.

"That too," Velvet said with a sigh. "That too."

# CHAPTER TWENTY-ONE

Velvet stepped off of the bus and walked down the street towards her flat, feeling both exhausted yet hopeful after spending the afternoon coming up with outlandish theories on Au's plans with Aria. She didn't think they had come close to working out what the Zubenelgenubian was up to, and she really hoped that she was right in thinking that Gold and the others would be arriving on Thursday.

She had really thought that if they stayed there long enough, intermittently pausing in conversation to energetically call to their friends, that one of them would come. But no one did.

She and Aria had now exchanged landline phone numbers. Velvet's old neighbour still had a landline, and had offered to take messages, and Aria's housemate was something of a doomsday prepper, and had refused to let their landlord shut down the landline. Aria promised she would call if any of the others turned up at the park, but Velvet already felt a restlessness in her bones at the idea of not having anything to do for the next few days, than to wait.

She reached her building and unlocked the door, then went upstairs to her flat. She really didn't feel like cooking, but was trying to eat what she had in her cupboards and save the little cash that she had left for emergencies. She needed to do a stock check of her food, to make sure she had enough to last until the Solstice, when hopefully everything would be back up, and she could access her money again.

In her tiny kitchenette, she filled the kettle with water (giving thanks for the fact that water and electric still appeared to be functioning) and switched it onto boil while she got a teabag and mug out of the cupboard.

After realising that Gold and the others might be on their way, she hadn't allowed herself to think about being reunited with Laguz so soon. But now as she waited for the water to boil, she felt her heart rate pick up at the idea of being with him again. She hadn't long left him, but it already felt like a lifetime.

She wondered if he would walk in to Greg's body again, as he had in his last human incarnation. She closed her eyes and imagined that he was stood behind her now, his arms wrapped around her waist, his chin resting gently on her shoulder, as he used to do, in their Seventh Dimension home, while she manifested their snacks of choice.

She sighed and melted into his embrace, and felt his breath in her ear.

"Look in the back of the bottom cupboard," he whispered.

Velvet's eyes snapped open and the feeling of his embrace disappeared. "Bottom cupboard?" she muttered to herself. She immediately leaned down and opened the cupboard doors, and started pulling out the contents. She had emptied the third one before she came across an old radio, tucked away at the back. She opened the battery compartment and was relieved to find it empty. Pulling some new batteries from her junk drawer, she jammed them in and then switched on the radio, twiddling the dials until she heard static.

She kept twisting until she could hear snippets of dialogue, and her heart leapt at the idea of being able to get news from the outside world more readily than relying on newspapers. She kept twisting the dial until suddenly a very familiar melody erupted loudly from the small device, making her jump.

Seconds later, she gasped at the shock of cold water lapping over her toes. She looked around and saw that she was on the beach near her home with Laguz.

"I knew you could hear me."

She spun around and dropped the radio on the sand. She ran towards Laguz and launched herself into his arms. He laughed and caught her, holding her tightly to his chest. She looked up at him and he leaned down to kiss her gently.

"How is this possible?" she asked.

"Our song, it will connect us always," he replied, nodding towards the discarded radio that was still softly playing the moonlight sonata, which could just about be heard over the waves crashing onto the golden sand.

"What's going on?" Velvet asked quickly, afraid that once the song ended, her Flame would disappear. "Why is the internet down? There's no phone signal either, what's happening?"

"Bk reset the internet and all the networks. It was the only way to reboot the walk-in program, to allow more of us to come and assist."

"Us? Are you coming? On the Solstice?" Velvet asked

hopefully tightening her arms around his waist.

"There is an army of Earth Angels ready to come, including all of the Children."

Velvet gasped. "The Children? They're all coming? How?"

"Starlight went to them, and asked them to come."

Velvet smiled. "Is my sister coming too?"

Laguz shook his head. "No, she plans to return to the stars. She is most unhappy with Gold. Though I will let him know that you got his message. I knew you would work out the reference."

Velvet chuckled. "You know what a *Lord of the Rings* fan I am."

Laguz rested his head on the top of hers and they were quiet for a moment, listening to the waves and the faint notes of Beethoven's movement.

"Just hang in there," Laguz whispered. "The Earth Angels and Children will be with you soon, and you can face this alien together."

"I can't wait," Velvet replied, breathing in his scent and lifting her head up to kiss him. Seconds after their lips met, the song ended, and she found herself standing in her kitchen again, holding the radio that was now crackling with static.

She turned the dial on the radio to switch it off and set it down on the counter. She poured hot water onto her teabag and then went into the living room and sat down.

She sipped her tea, completely oblivious to the liquid burning her mouth as she relived the last few moments spent in Laguz's arms on the beach.

He was coming. Gold was coming. The Children were coming. And together, they would save the world. Again.

It had been an excruciatingly long three days, because Velvet had stayed in her flat the whole time. By the third day of the outage, unrest was breaking out, and the Army had been called upon to keep the peace. Shops were being looted, there were protests and riots in the streets, and it didn't feel safe to be outside.

Aria had called and left a couple of messages, to say that some of the Earth Angels had turned up at the park. It was going to be tricky getting there and gathering though, because there was a curfew in place and people had been instructed to stay in their homes.

But nothing was going to stop Velvet from going to the park that evening. The thought of seeing her Flame again was the only thing keeping her going.

The busses no longer ran after 6pm, so Velvet had borrowed a bike from a neighbour, and she had packed a rucksack with the remaining food she had, and a blanket. She and Aria planned to camp out in the park and wait for dawn. Velvet was very glad it was Solstice and that dawn would come early, and it wouldn't be too cold outside.

She was so excited to see Laguz again, that she had barely slept over the previous seventy-two hours. There was a small voice in the back of her head, warning her not to get too excited, because when she considered his words, he hadn't specifically said he was coming, but surely he would be? Why wouldn't he?

Velvet gathered her things, then walked the bike to the lift, and exited onto the street, carefully checking around for any patrols. Luckily, her area seemed to be largely unmanned, and she hopped on the bike and rode quietly down the pavement, silently calling out to the Angels to protect her and make her invisible to any prying eyes.

It took over an hour to get there, and on the way she wondered if Gold really would be coming to Earth, and whether he and the other Earth Angels now had a solution to all of the chaos Au had caused. She knew she should have been focussing on coming up with solutions as well, but as soon as she realised everyone was coming, she felt less pressure to work it all out and have all the answers. Because truthfully, she had none. She was no closer to working out what Au's plans were, or what could possibly be worse than the wars, plagues and famines she had already facilitated. She wondered whether Tim had managed to find the Starpeople and convince them to help. Aria hadn't had any communications from him, and Velvet knew that Aria was hoping that he would be one of the ones arriving at dawn.

By the time she arrived at the park, Velvet was feeling quite drained. But her energy picked up when she approached the bench where she and Aria had planned to meet and saw several shadows of people amongst candles burning in jars.

"Velvet's here!" she heard one of them exclaim, before rushing forwards to greet her.

"Oh, Beryl! It's so good to see you." Velvet propped the bike up then hugged her friend tightly. Velvet was relieved to see that so many had now come, and she gratefully took the food offered, having been living on the contents of her cupboards for the last three days.

They discussed the messages they had received, and the prophecy of the Return of the Earth Angels (a rather fancy title that Amethyst had given what they hoped to soon experience).

Too many of them had received similar messages for it to be a coincidence, and Velvet was confident that come dawn, they would be seeing many of their old friends again.

Time crept by slowly, and Velvet kept checking her phone for the time, but the minutes crawled past, even though she was having such fun. She knew it was because she so desperately wanted to be in Laguz's arms again, to kiss his lips for real, not just in a vision. And because she wanted to prove the nagging, doubtful little voice wrong.

After a couple of hours, the conversation had died down, and the others were quietly meditating, or in the case of the little green Faerie, curled up on a blanket snoring softly. It appeared that the park was not patrolled by the Army, and indeed, Velvet had not seen a single patrol on the whole journey there. So either things had calmed enough to not need their presence, or the Angels were protecting her and the others from being seen. Either way, she felt like she could relax a little.

Velvet lay back on her own blanket and stared up at the stars twinkling through the tree branches above them. She saw a shooting star, and wondered if it was Tim, shooting across the galaxy in his ship. Just in case it wasn't, and it really was a star, she made a silent wish, then closed her eyes.

*   *   *

"Velvet!"

Had Velvet not been so stiff from sleeping on the ground, she would have sat bolt upright, but the best she could manage was a groan and rolling onto her side. "What?" she mumbled, trying to open her eyes.

"It's dawn," the voice said excitedly.

Velvet's eyes popped open and she pushed herself into a sitting position, wincing at the dampness of the dew on her clothing and her blanket. There was light in the sky, and there was a hazy pink glow all around them. The other Earth Angels were all stirring. Velvet pulled out her phone and checked the time. It was exactly 4.44am. She smiled at the angel number.

She hadn't been asleep long, but she suddenly felt very awake and alert, her heart was pounding in her ears in the quiet, which was only broken by birdsong.

"Are they here?" Magenta asked, looking around them.

Velvet stood up slowly, her limbs aching and her joints creaking. She looked around the park but couldn't see anyone else. She shook her head. "I don't think so, of course, that's assuming we are in the right place."

"We must be!" Aria insisted. "Because surely wherever we are is the right place? They would come to us. Makes no sense not to."

Velvet nodded at the Faerie's wise words. "Indeed, I agree. But the messages did all say dawn, and well, dawn is here." She was trying not to lose heart, but it was difficult, when she so very much needed to see her Flame.

"They will be here," Amethyst said, rising to her feet and picking up her blanket, folding it neatly and placing it in her bag. The others followed suit, putting away their blankets and the food, and tidying up the site.

Velvet put her bag on the bench, and stretched her arms over her head, trying to get the stiffness out of her body. It had been some time since she had been camping, she wasn't used to it.

"What do you think will happen? Once they arrive?"

Aria asked. "Will they really have a plan to fix everything?"

Velvet sighed. "I have no idea, but I really do hope that they have a plan. Because I am at a loss. Unless we find Au or figure out her plan, I don't know how we can fix everything that she has done."

"Maybe Tim has found a way," Aria said hopefully, pushing her straggly blonde hair out of her eyes and shivering slightly in her thin jacket.

Velvet pulled out an extra jumper from her bag and handed it to the Faerie, who took it with a grateful grin and put it on underneath her jacket.

"Thanks, Velvet. I guess I didn't prepare for the cold. It was so warm yesterday."

"You're welcome," Velvet said, sitting next to her on the bench. "Come on, Laguz, where are you?" she muttered, scanning the trees around them.

A moment later, a glint of sunlight broke through the tree and shone onto her face, and she heard Magenta gasp. She got up and spun around, and her hand flew to her mouth as she heard the Faerie gasp next to her.

With each ray of sunlight that filtered through the trees, a soul appeared before them, one, and then another, then another, until the park was filled with Earth Angels and Children, all bathed in the bright light of the rising sun.

Tears filled Velvet's eyes at the beautiful sight, as she scanned their faces, recognising many, but not seeing the one she most needed to see.

As the final ray shone through, Gold materialised just a few steps away from her. Their eyes met, and before he shook his head ever so slightly, the twitch in his right eye told her everything she needed to know.

Her Flame was not coming.

# CORDUROY

## CHAPTER TWENTY-TWO

"I thought I might find you here."

Corduroy looked up at the Head of Guardian Angels and shrugged. "Guess I have become predictable of late."

Athena smiled and joined him on the bench in the Atlantis Garden that faced the marble statues of Velvet and Laguz. "Nothing wrong with a little predictability. Though I imagine after twenty years of living the same day, a little bit of spontaneity wouldn't go amiss either."

Corduroy sighed. "I still don't see why we couldn't go to Earth. Why we couldn't help Velvet and the others."

Athena raised an eyebrow at the Old Soul. "Help them? You mean find Au and get revenge?"

Corduroy knew it was pointless to protest. "Are you not angry too? You were frozen for twenty years. Do you not wish for justice?"

"I wish for peace," Athena said gently. "What Au has done is wrong, but she was doing it for reasons she thought were right. What we did, creating and allowing the loop to exist, was wrong, but we did it for reasons we thought were right. How are we so different to Au? If she needs to be brought to justice, do we not also? We have played a part in all of this too."

Corduroy hated that the Angel was right, and in a way, he realised that was why his need for justice, for revenge against the alien, was so strong. It was being fed by his guilt for the part he had played in the whole debacle. He knew he was to blame for creating the loop. Every man, woman and child who had suffered because of the alien, was in fact, suffering because of him.

And he needed to make it right.

"It's not your responsibility to right all of the wrongs," Athena said softly, surely reading his mind, or at least, reading his silence. "You were not the only one involved. But just as Bk is playing his part here, and Gold is now also, on Earth, we must also play our parts in ensuring that Au is found, reined in, and the damage limited or if possible, reversed."

"And how do we do that from here?" Corduroy asked, frustrated. "We are unable to contact Velvet and the others on Earth, and we have searched for signs of Au, but have not found her. We are relying on Tm to find the other Zubenelgenubians and for the army of light we have sent to start reversing the damage." He knew that getting annoyed with the Angel was pointless, but he really hated feeling useless. And in that moment, he really couldn't see the point of him being there, when he could do nothing at all.

"Let's go and see Bk and Laguz, they may need our help or have ideas of what we can do to assist the Earth Angels on Earth."

"Fine," Corduroy sighed. He held out his hand, and Athena took it. A click later, they vanished from the Atlantis Garden.

"I'm so sorry, Laguz, Gold shouldn't have insisted you stay."

Corduroy and Athena reappeared in the operations room, startling Laguz and the Angel of Destiny.

"Starlight," Corduroy said, surprised. "I thought you had returned to the stars."

"She came to see why I had not gone to Earth," Laguz said. He shook his head. "I have made my peace with it, even if I do not like it."

Corduroy felt a small amount of glee spark up in his soul. Though upset that he was not on Earth with his old love, his oldest friend at that moment, it gave him comfort knowing that neither was his fish-tailed foe.

Starlight sighed. "I only hope that Gold was considering the bigger picture when he asked you to stay, and not just his own interests. Anyway, I shall be returning to the stars now, I have much to do, and quite honestly, I cannot bear witness to the outcome of the madness that Gold has created."

"Gold wasn't the only one who created this," Bk interjected, looking up from the control panel where he had been quietly working alongside Dahlia, who was unusually quiet.

"There are many of us to blame," Corduroy agreed.

Athena murmured her agreement.

Starlight shrugged. "Well may this be on all of you to sort out. I would wish you luck, but well, I don't think it will help." She smiled at Laguz. "Give my best to my sister, for I am certain the two of you shall be reunited soon."

Laguz smiled back. "Thank you, I do hope so."

With another sigh, there was a flash of light and Starlight disappeared, leaving behind a cloud of stardust and twinkling lights.

"If the Angel of Destiny has given up on us, and on Earth, surely we are done for?" Corduroy said miserably to no one in particular.

"She called upon the Children to help, and has assisted us thus far. I don't believe she has given up," Athena said thoughtfully. "I think she is just upset that Gold put his own needs above hers, again, and they shall never again reunite. Lost love does funny things to a soul."

Corduroy caught Laguz's eye, and for a moment the men shared an understanding of that very same pain. If they weren't in love with the same woman, they might have been friends. Maybe, in an alternate dimension somewhere, they were.

"I'm not giving up," Bk said determinedly. "I believe that there must be a way to stop Au from causing further damage, and I won't rest until I figure out how."

"We are with you," Athena said. "What can we do to help?"

# CHAPTER TWENTY-THREE

Corduroy was sat at his desk, feeling both exhausted and energised by the mixture of hope and rage within him. Despite the calm influence of Athena, he had been struggling to stop his bitterness from spilling out, and now that he was finally alone, he allowed the dark thoughts to crash around his mind, a kaleidoscope of hate and fear and anger.

He should have pushed them to destroy the machine before all of the Earth Angels had returned. He could see now that it was the only way that Au could be stopped from completing her grand plan. Which they still had no idea what it was.

But now Velvet was there, on Earth. Would the destruction of the machine make her disappear, as his students had when they stopped the loop at the Academy?

He still wasn't entirely sure how it all worked. If Au had gone back in time to the actual reality of the Diamond Age, then that wasn't a loop, so destroying the machine wouldn't make humans disappear. Would it?

He let out a growl of frustration. If only he actually

understood it all, how the machine worked, how the loops worked and what Au had done to the machine to sabotage it. Then maybe he would be of more use to Bk and the others. Instead, he just felt an overwhelming rage simmering under the surface, which had been dormant for a long time.

It had been reignited when he saw Velvet.

But why? Because she had not loved him as he loved her? Because he was not her Flame? Because she looked so damned beautiful it made his heart ache?

Without really thinking, stood up and clicked his fingers. He reappeared in the hidden room where the machine was whirring away. He was surprised to find it unattended and the door closed. But perhaps the others were taking a much needed break. The hour was late, and they had been working on a solution to this mess nonstop.

The Old Soul took the seat in front of the machine, and started pressing buttons at random, trying to remember what he had seen Laguz and Bk doing. For the first time in his long existence, he wished he was more of a tech geek, but alas, advanced technology held little interest to him. He did know that this machine was quite different to the one in Atlantis, though it bore similarities having also been created by Starpeople.

He was about to dig around to see if he could find out how to shut the machine down, when he heard a noise over his shoulder.

"Corduroy? What are you doing here?"

The Old Soul sighed and without looking replied, "Good evening, Laguz." The suspicion in the Merman's voice had raised his hackles, and it took a lot of effort to not just click his fingers and disappear.

Corduroy heard Laguz enter the room and come

to stand next to him. He glanced up to see the Merman scanning the machine to see what was amiss. "Really, what are you doing?"

Corduroy shrugged. "I just wanted to understand. I wanted to be useful. I wanted to make a fucking difference. I'm tired of being the bad guy. But mostly, I'm angry. At myself, at Au, at the universe." He hadn't intended on unleashing his innermost thoughts, but he couldn't help it, the rage was beginning to boil over.

He felt a hand on his shoulder, and though he wanted to shrink away from Laguz's touch, there was something solid and grounding about it.

"Sabotaging or shutting down the machine is not the answer. We have considered it, and it will not work. I understand that you want revenge against Au. Believe me, I'm angry too. But this is not the way. It was not the way in Atlantis, and it is not the way now."

His calm, even tone was irritating, but oddly soothing. Corduroy had expected Laguz's ire, not his compassion. After all, he was to blame for Laguz losing his Flame, again.

Before he could reply, Laguz continued.

"I think it is time you go and find your Flame. I think her presence would calm you, and right now, you need to balance your anger with love. Because the humans, the Earth Angels, and the Children do not need any more anger. You are hurting them more than helping them by being here."

His words stabbed at Corduroy's soul like small icicles of cold hard truth. He nodded, because there was nothing more he could say. Laguz was right. His darkness was not going to overcome the darkness on Earth. It could only add to it. Velvet needed the light. Earth needed the light.

And Corduroy needed the light. He knew that if he let

his rage take hold, Athena was also right, he would become as bad as Au. Just another spark of light overcome by the darkness.

He thought of his Flame. She had not recognised him the last time he had gone to her. But perhaps he could remind her who he was and what they had experienced together. Thinking of his Flame started to lighten his energy, and it seemed that Laguz sensed the slight shift, as he squeezed his shoulder, then let go.

Corduroy stood up, looked the Merman in his sparkling green eyes one more time, then he clicked his fingers and set the intention to return to his Flame.

And return to the light.

# TM

## CHAPTER TWENTY-FOUR

Tm sat at the controls of the spacecraft, familiarising himself with the tech that he had once helped to develop, eons ago. He made a note of the upgrades that Bk had made, glad that he had such a skilled Starperson on his side.

He was doing his best to focus on the task at hand, but he was struggling to get the image of Aria out of his mind. Despite not being Flames, they had loved each other and cared for each other for a whole lifetime on Earth. To leave her there again after such a short reunion felt more painful than leaving his Flame in the Eighth Dimension, thinking it would only be for a brief time.

He shook his head, trying to bring himself back to the present moment. He considered dropping in to see his Flame first, before beginning his mission, but he knew that if he saw her, he would not want to leave her again. So it was best to wait until he was done, and then he would never leave her side again.

He might also see if Aria and Linen wanted to join them in the Eighth, so that all his favourite people were in the same realm again.

Unable to put off leaving any longer, Tm got the spacecraft ready for flight, and was about to turn back into his light body in order to fly, when he saw a figure on the monitor, by the door of the craft. Frowning, he hit the button to open the door, and turned to see Bk enter the craft.

"Bk, is everything okay? I know I should have left already, I was just, um," he waved half-heartedly at the controls, but then shrugged. "Procrastinating, really."

Bk nodded. "Understandable, you have quite the mission ahead, are you sure you're up to it?"

Tm sighed. "Yes, I can do it. I need to do it. I have felt so hopeless these last twenty-three years, and I'm so, *so* sorry I didn't do more to ensure that you realised sooner."

Bk waved his hand dismissively. "Forget about it. I imagine it was much worse for you, knowing what was going on. We were blissfully ignorant of anything amiss."

"Thank you. Now, what can I do for you?"

Bk was quiet for a moment. "You are the only other Starperson I can speak to right now, so I needed your opinion before I ask Starlight and Gold."

Tm nodded. "Sure, on what?"

"I think that in order to get the walk-in program back online, I need to kill the internet."

Tm raised an eyebrow. "Kill it? As in...?"

"Take it offline. Globally. Potentially lose all the data. Pretty sure the mobile phone networks will also go down, maybe some satellites too."

"Ah. Well. Umm, okay." Tm was quiet for a moment while his mind considered the ramifications of this action. After a few moments, he sighed. "I don't know. It would change the world completely, as it currently relies so heavily on the internet in particular. It might have apocalyptic consequences."

Bk sighed. "That's what I'm afraid of. That in trying to save the world, we might accidentally end it."

"Is there no other way? And is the walk-in program important enough to risk it?" Tm didn't voice the fact that he had assumed the walk-in program was dead and that he wouldn't have to return to Earth. What if they asked him to go back?

Bk sat on the stool next to Tm and put his head in his hands. "I have run so many scenarios through the machine, through my mind, and I honestly just don't know at this point, what the best thing to do is. And I need to do the best thing, because all of this is my fault."

"Well, not all of it," Tm said. "It was Gold's idea to give the humans more chances."

"And I created the tech to make it happen. I should have known that it would cause ripples that would be bad."

"Au was a complete anomaly," Tm argued. "No one could have seen that coming, the darkness that she would bring."

Bk sighed. "I feel like I should have. But I thought Zubenelgenubi was doing okay. I had no idea it had died. Imagine that? Not even knowing that your home is gone?"

Tm shook his head. "I didn't know either. It's not your fault. You cannot shoulder the blame for all this and hope to have enough light energy to solve it. Let the blame go. It is time."

Bk nodded. "Thank you. Now, any thoughts?"

"I'm sorry, I just don't know. I mean, the old 'switch it off then on again' protocol has generally always worked in the past."

"Except this is more like switching it off, shaking it upside down for several days, then switching it back on again," Bk said with a grim chuckle.

Tm smiled at his kin. "True. But that has also worked in the past. Though in this case, there may be consequences that we cannot see now, that could make things worse." Tm swallowed his fear of being asked to return to Earth, and added, "But if the humans are lost without the Earth Angels returning to Earth en masse, then I think you will just have to do it and hope for the best."

Bk nodded. "I think you're right. And I do think that they need to return. It is only the light that they can bring that will change everything."

Tm smiled. "I know you will do everything you can to make things right, and I will do what I can too. If I can find the Zubenelgenubians who Au has been controlling, then they will be able to put an end to all of this." *And my role in this will be over,* he added silently.

"Good luck," Bk said, standing up and holding out his hand to shake Tm's.

"You too, my friend, my brother."

Bk nodded and moved to the door, which opened to allow him to exit. But before the door could close again, Tm saw another being approach. He frowned, trying to figure out who they were. The soul squeezed Bk's arm as they passed him, then they stepped up onto the craft.

Tm frowned. "I know you, but I don't remember."

The soul smiled. "I am Jr, and this is my craft. I heard through the ether that you might be in need of a co-pilot."

Tm grinned, feeling like something might finally be going right.

"Jr, it's so good to see you again!" He stood up and

threw his arms around his fellow Zubenelgenubian, one of the most experienced pilots from his home planet.

"Shall we get this show on the road?" she asked, grinning. Tm nodded and the two Starpeople sat at the controls, and once the door was safely closed, they turned into their light forms, fired up the craft, and lifted up from the dock.

Within light-seconds, they were shooting through the universe, leaving the Earth Angel Training Academy far behind.

*   *   *

Tm and Jr flew in companionable silence for many light years. Stars and galaxies spun past them, creating the best light show anyone might ever have experienced in the universe.

Had Tm had a human body still, he might have been moved to tears by the sheer beauty of it all, by the depth of the potential that still remained, even after so many millions of years.

"You know where they are? The Zubenelgenubians we seek?" he communicated to Jr, realising that she was steering them in a very particular direction.

"Yes," she replied, her words appearing in his being, not as words but as feelings, intentions. "Many of them left this galaxy for another, I think they needed a change."

"I am saddened that none returned to our home."

Tm felt Jr's sigh, her sadness at the mention of their planet. Her light dimmed just a little.

"They knew that it was dark now, but they did not know that Au remained there. Only I knew. I had hoped she would follow us, and so I left her this craft. I had no idea the darkness would infect her so badly, that it would make her do such evil things to those on Earth.”

Tm reached his light arm towards her, his light blending with hers, lifting her up. “You are not to blame, just as Bk is not to blame. No one could have known. It is not in our nature to think such dark things, to create such evil. To want revenge, it is unfathomable.”

Jr’s sadness prevailed through their connection, making Tm sad too. “I still think I could have done more. So I will atone for my actions or lack thereof by helping you, and Velvet, and Gold. I will do whatever I can to be of service.”

“I appreciate your help,” Tm replied. “I would have been searching the universe blindly, looking for their energy. You are ensuring that we find them much sooner, and hopefully put an end to the chaos on Earth much sooner too.”

Jr’s light brightened just a fraction, and Tm returned his light to the control panel. “How long until we arrive?”

“We have many more light years to go. I see that Bk has upgraded the craft. Shall we use the boosters now? It will shorten our outward trip considerably, but may mean that the return trip may take a little longer.”

“Let’s boost it, we can always find a faster way to return if needed.”

Tm felt Jr’s assent, and she pushed a button with her light hand then pulled a lever all the way towards her, and suddenly the stars rushing past them all began to blend together, creating the sensation of rushing through a light tunnel, but instead of light at the end of it, there was only a tiny dot of unknown darkness.

* * *

"Jr, are you seeing this?"

After many more light years of the star tunnel, the horizon had suddenly turned a bright purple, but instead of the one line, there were two, parallel to one another, and they were rushing forwards into the gap in-between which had a green hue.

"Yes," Jr responded. "We are close."

Suddenly, they were inside the green band of light, but Tm could see now that it was not one band of light, but in fact many separate lights, that were actually-

"Numbers?" Tm queried, feeling confused as the digits rushed past them. There didn't appear to be any pattern to them that he could discern, but they were moving at a very fast pace.

"The very thing that the entire universe is made from."

"So we are headed into the source? The very centre of the universe?"

"Yes, we are headed to infinity."

Tm watched the numbers flying past for a short while before communicating again. "Why did they come here? Was this further sabotage? Surely, from here they could control the whole universe? Have they become dark, like Au?"

Tm could feel Jr's surprise at his words. "No, I don't think that's the case at all. You know what we Zubenelgenubians are like, we are drawn to the light, we are fascinated by the possibilities of the universe. They came here to learn, to evolve, to understand, to help."

"But how do you know that?" Tm asked, still uncertain. He hated doubting his co-pilot, and doubting his kin. But spending time with Au had shown him that even the lightest of souls could turn dark.

Jr paused just a little too long before responding, and Tm's fears expanded.

"I cannot be certain," she said finally. "But I know that was their intent, or at least, that was the intent they communicated before they left. I just hope that it remained their intent, and that they have not been aiding Au's plans all this time."

Tm's fears did not abate, but he noticed that the numbers appeared to be getting denser and the green light was getting brighter and brighter, until it shone so brightly that it engulfed them both and their craft.

# CHAPTER TWENTY-FIVE

It is one thing to have no physical form, to be a being of light in a world of form. But to be a being of light, in the midst of light, where there are no boundaries, no shape, no form, no matter, and no time or even space, was an entirely different matter.

Tm could barely tell where he existed, or where Jr was either. Their craft didn't appear to exist either. How would they leave? He was glad at least that he still appeared to be capable of thought, which meant that he did, in fact, still exist, but how would he find the others? Or Jr? Was this a trap? Had Jr betrayed him? Was she trying to stop him from completing his mission and helping the humans?

"Tm."

Hearing his name from Jr in an ethereal whisper, so softly and calmly, stopped his mind spiralling out of control for a moment.

"All is well, Tm, you are allowing your human mind to take over, let go and allow the light to enter you."

For a moment Tm felt embarrassed, clearly his thoughts had been communicated to Jr, and whoever else might be in the light with them.

"Matters not, let go of your human emotions and let the light in," Jr coaxed gently.

It felt like it took a huge amount of effort to let all his doubts, fears and emotions go, but indeed, the effort was also a human construct that had no place here in the light. So without any further thought, Tm relaxed every particle of his being, and became one with the light.

*　*　*

"Tm, welcome, it is most delightful to see you again."

"Mg! You are here too? It has been so many eons since our paths last crossed."

"Indeed, it has been. What brings you to the light?"

Though the light was all encompassing, Tm could sense the souls of other beings nearby, and he tuned into them, one by one, recognising their light bodies.

"Al, Mo, Si, Fi, Ra, Li, Ti! You are all here. You are the ones we have been searching for."

"We are?" Al enquired. "Whatever for?"

Knowing that they didn't have any more time to waste, after all, how much time would have passed on Earth by now? Tm connected his light energy to theirs and in a few microseconds, transferred everything he knew of Au's plan and all that had happened on Earth and in the Fifth Dimension in the last few decades.

Their shock and dismay as they understood caused the green light to dim and spark haphazardly, showering them in a cascade of random numbers and making things a little confusing for a second.

It was the calming energy of Mg that brought things

back to order.

"This is quite unexpected," Mg said, his energy sad, but doing its best to stay bright. "What can we do?"

"We need Al and the others to return to their Earthly bodies," Jr said. "They are the ones whose technology has created the chaos. And they have been doing Au's bidding all this time. They need to take control of their Earthly counterparts and help us to end the dark times."

"How did we not know they were doing this? If they are using our Earth bodies? How did we not hear the call to return?" Mo asked, still emanating shock.

"Au has evolved beyond our comprehension. What she has done, what she has created, and what she has yet to wreak upon the human race, is beyond our imagination. The darkness that took hold of her is beyond what we can understand."

Though he didn't say anything, Tm could feel the regret from Mg. Because like him, he felt responsible for leaving Au there, for allowing her to be abandoned on a dying planet.

"There's nothing you could have done differently," he communicated quietly, directing his words for Mg only.

Mg acknowledged his words, but Tm could tell that he didn't fully agree. "What should I do? I have no Earthly body. Am I of use?"

"I think you need to stay here," Jr said, surprising Tm, who was about to say that he should return with them also, that perhaps he could be of help to Bk, with the machine that Au had hacked.

"What am I to do here? I am of no use to you this far away?"

"I think I have a way of staying in touch," Jr said. "I just get the feeling that we need someone here, with whom we can contact."

Mg seemed to be as confused as Tm felt, but he assented to Jr's view. "Very well. Will you all be leaving presently?"

"The present is all that exists," Jr responded, though not in a sarcastic tone.

Almost as soon as her response was felt, Tm found himself rushing backwards, and Mg's energy slipped away before Tm could communicate a proper farewell.

Within moments, he was engulfed by green numbers rushing past, though this time they were rushing ahead as he rushed backwards. Not many moments later, it seemed, Tm found himself able to discern his own light body again. Then Jr's light body. Then moments later, the craft reappeared around them, and Tim and Jr took control of the craft as they whizzed away from the purple horizons, the green numbers turning back into a single band of light and colour.

"Everyone present and correct?" Jr communicated into the back of the craft.

Tm turned to see the seven light bodies of his fellow Zubenelgenubians all hovering behind him, and his own light swelled.

They had done it. They had found the seven, and now they could return to the Academy, and save planet Earth.

# CHAPTER TWENTY-SIX

When the craft docked outside the Earth Angel Training Academy, Tm set the intention for his human body to return, and looked over to Jr to see her do the same.

He looked behind him to see the seven light beings also take on their human form, and Tm looked at each face, seeing the seven powerful men that he had been studying on Earth for the last twenty years. That he and Jr had found them, and they were all willing to return to Earth to save the humans from the darkness, felt like nothing short of a miracle.

He only hoped that they weren't too late.

He looked over at Jr. "I do hope we're not too late," he said, voicing his fears out loud.

Jr smiled at him. "We have just been to infinity and back, and you think it's possible for us to be late?"

Tm frowned, and followed her off the craft as the door swung open. Their seven kin followed suit, and they made their way into the Academy, to the operations room.

When the door disappeared and they entered the room, Tm saw Bk sat at the main control panel, the pink Faerie,

Dahlia, busy at his side. He cleared his throat and the Starperson and Faerie looked up to see the nine of them, and the Faerie fell off her stool with a squeak before using her wings to catch herself at the last moment.

Bk stood up and stared at them, taking in their faces one by one. "You all came," he said simply, the shock evident on his face.

"Is it too late?" Tm asked, slightly desperately. "Did it take us too long?"

Bk chuckled. "Too long? Tm, you only left hours ago. Gold and the other Earth Angels only left moments ago, you just missed them."

Tm's eyes widened and he glanced at Jr who was grinning.

"But, but how is that possible? We travelled for light years! We went all the way to infinity..."

"And beyond?" Bk joked. "I guess my upgrades worked then."

"Perfectly," Jr responded. "It's a shame we have missed the others, but I assume you can send us all back into our own bodies immediately?"

"All except Tm, yes, as he doesn't exist in this timeline. But the walk-in program is running now, so I can send him as he is."

Tm's heart sank. "Oh, I'm going back? Am I needed?" He looked at Jr and Bk, praying one of them would say no.

"Oh," Bk said. "I just assumed that you would be going back with the seven, to stop Au, but, well, it's up to you, no one is being forced to go."

Tm knew that Bk wasn't trying to guilt him into going, but he felt guilty nevertheless. He felt Jr touch his arm.

"You can stay," she said softly. "You have done enough."

Tm shook his head. "No, Bk is right, I should see this through. I will return." Even though the thought of it made him feel sick, the idea of seeing Aria in her human incarnation again raised his spirits slightly.

"Bk, I think I need your..." Laguz's words trailed off as he entered the room from the hidden machine room and he saw all the Zubenelgenubians there. "Holy shit," he said. "That was fast!"

"Laguz?" Tm said, confused. "I thought you would have returned to Earth with the others? To be with Velvet?"

Laguz sighed, his face clouded over. "It's a long story. But congratulations on completing your mission! Quite impressive."

"Thanks, I had help," Tm said, glancing at Jr. "So, when do we go?"

Bk went back to the control panel and studied the screens for a moment. "Give me an hour?"

Tm nodded. "We will be in the gardens. You can call me and I will gather everyone to the main hall."

"Perfect, thanks."

Tm turned and herded his fellow Starpeople out the door. "Explore, go wherever you want in the Academy, I will call you."

They each nodded and headed off in the direction of the gardens. "Where are you headed?" Jr asked, intuitively picking up that he had no intention of joining them for a stroll.

Tm bit his lip. He hadn't intended on letting anyone know, but he knew he could trust Jr. "I need to see my Flame. I don't know how long I will have to be on Earth, and I cannot bear the fact that I have left her for so long already. I figured I could get there in the craft and be back before I had even left?"

Jr smiled. "I will take you."

Tm smiled back. "Thank you."

"Let's go."

*   *   *

The Eighth Dimension home that Tm shared with his Flame, Hannah, was dark when he and Jr arrived and docked the craft outside.

"How long do I have?" Tm asked his co-pilot and now co-conspirator.

Jr winked at him. "Take all the time you need, I can get you back before either of us is missed."

Tm smiled gratefully. "Thank you."

He slipped out of his seat and exited the craft, and despite Jr's words, found himself running up to his home, desperate to spend as many moments with his Flame as he could.

He opened the front door, feeling slightly out of breath, though such a thing wasn't normal in the Eighth Dimension. His human programming was taking over. He caught his breath and then silently ran up the stairs to where he hoped to find his Flame.

When he reached their bedroom door, he paused for a moment, scared that he might be rebuffed, that his beloved Indigo might have moved on. Or that she would never be able to forgive him for being gone a lifetime.

Finally, knowing that time was precious, he took a deep breath and pushed the door open. He went in and saw Hannah's sleeping form under the covers, and his heart started to pound. He went over to his side of the bed, and slipped off his shoes and slid under the covers next to his Flame. She murmured something in her sleep, so he shifted closer to her, before kissing her gently on the forehead.

Her eyes flew open, and met his, completely alert and awake. Sleep wasn't necessary in the Eighth Dimension, but it was still something they enjoyed doing.

"Tim?" she whispered, reaching out to touch his face. "Is it really you?"

Tm pressed her fingers against his face with his hand. "Yes, my love, I'm here, I'm so sorry I was gone so long."

Tears filled Hannah's eyes and she kissed him hard. "Where have you been all this time?" she asked, her voice a little louder now. She sat up and waved her hand at the bedside lamp, which lit the room with a dull yellow glow.

Tm sat up next to her, his body turned towards her, as he clasped her hands in his. "I was on Earth. The call I felt was to re-enter my body when it was in the Earth Angel Training Academy." He sighed. "It's all such a complicated tale, and I promise I will tell you all of it, but I don't have the time right now, because I cannot stay."

Hannah frowned and her hands gripped his. "What? You're not staying? You're not home now for good?"

Tm shook his head. "Jr is waiting in a craft outside for me, we are returning to the Academy, and then returning to Earth. There is a situation that needs my attention, I must see it through."

"Earth? But I thought there was no one there? I don't understand?"

Tm sighed. "And I promise I will explain, but I don't want to spend this short time I have with you talking, I wish to hold you and be with you, and imprint the memory of your lips on mine so that I can get through whatever challenges come next."

Hannah's frown softened and she sighed. "I have missed you so," she said, leaning towards him to kiss him. She held her lips on his for the longest time, and he melted into her embrace, kissing her again and again with more passion than he had felt for the previous two decades.

Soon, all thoughts of Jr waiting for him and returning to Earth had left his mind, as he lost himself in his Flame.

# CHAPTER TWENTY-SEVEN

The early morning sunlight shone on Tm's face, waking him suddenly from a dreamless sleep. He sat bolt upright in the bed, and looked around, but Hannah wasn't there. It was morning already? How long had he been there? Jr! Was she still waiting outside?

He jumped up and nearly tripped over his clothing and the discarded covers on the floor. He looked out of the window to see the craft hovering patiently there, but it appeared to be empty.

He waved his hand at himself and intended to be dressed, and clothing appeared on his body, shoes on his feet. He then left the bedroom and headed down the stairs, and as he neared the kitchen, he heard voices.

He entered the sunny kitchen and found his Flame laughing and chatting with Jr.

"Jr! I am so sorry, why didn't you come to wake me? We only had an hour, will they have gone without us?"

Jr chuckled. "Hannah, your Flame has become quite the worrywart after his last Earthly incarnation." She bit into her toast and chased the mouthful down with some pomegranate juice. "Tm, I told you to take your time, and I meant it."

"Your lie in has given Jr the chance to fill me in," Hannah said, coming over to Tm and handing him a cup of coffee. She reached up on her tiptoes to kiss him. "It sounds like you had such an awful time. Is Earth really that bad now?"

Tm sipped the coffee that was the perfect drinking temperature and nodded. "Worse. She has created a hell on Earth, using our technology," he said nodding to Jr, whose smile slipped from her face.

"But we have found the seven now. And they will make things right. We just need to get them back to Earth, and join the others," Jr said.

"We must go," Tm said, putting his cup down.

"In a moment," Jr said, finishing her breakfast. "You need to take your time with this goodbye, for who knows how long it will take us to sort out the mess on Earth?" She got up and gave Hannah a hug. "Farewell, Indigo. I promise I will make sure he makes it back to you as soon as he can."

Hannah hugged the Starperson and smiled. "Thank you, and thank you for bringing him here now and for giving us this time."

Jr nodded and headed out of the kitchen and out of the house back towards the craft.

Tm looked at Hannah, who was busying herself with dishes at the sink. A farce, as there was no need to do any actual chores in the Eighth Dimension. But then, there was also no need to eat, it was just something they had enjoyed from their human lives.

"Hannah," Tm said, going over to his Flame and wrapping his arms around her waist from behind. He felt tears hit his arm and he sighed. "I'm so sorry to leave again so soon. Though I hadn't dared to hope to have a whole night with you, so that was an unexpected joy."

Hannah put the dishes down in the sink and turned to face him, burying her face in his chest. "Just do whatever you need to do, then come back to me? Okay? Because I need you here."

"I promise that I won't stay there a moment longer than necessary," Tm said, resting his chin on her head, breathing in her scent. "As soon as it seems that the chaos has been dealt with, and Earth is back on a positive trajectory, I will come back."

"I love you," Hannah whispered.

"I love you, too," Tm replied, tightening his arms around her, wishing that he could just stay there forever.

Hannah pulled away first, turning her back to him and starting to clean the dishes again.

Tm sighed and stepped away. "I'll be back soon," he said, as he walked slowly away.

"Til then," Hannah replied, not turning to watch him leave.

Tm nodded, and wiped his own tears away with the back of his hand. Before he could change his mind and beg his Flame to stop him from leaving, he left the kitchen, headed down the hall and out of the front door.

When he got back to the craft and sat at the controls, he felt Jr's gaze, but the wise Starperson said nothing, and instead fired up the craft and lifted them up into the air.

Tm couldn't bear to watch his home disappear behind them, and instead did his best to focus on the task immediately ahead of them.

*   *   *

"Tm, Jr, you are both right on time."

Tm glanced at Jr, who grinned back at him. He had no idea how she had done it, but she had got them back to the Academy minutes before Bk called to them to meet with the others in the main hall. He silently thanked Bk for upgrading the craft, then joined the seven Zubenelgenubians and Bk.

"So, the seven of you and Jr will be re-entering your Earth bodies, arriving shortly after the other Earth Angels, as we have managed to regain access to the time changing abilities of the machine. You have had the full briefing now, of the situation on Earth, and of your own lives, and hopefully you will figure out how to deescalate the situations that have been created, and create solutions to the issues humans now face."

"Not to mention work out Au's grand plan?" Mo said, his face grave. "Do we have any idea at all?"

Bk shook his head. "No, although if it has anything to do with the internet, we may have scuppered it somewhat, because I was only able to restore some of the data. Much was lost in the reboot."

"Which will also affect our lives," Fi said. "It seems that most of us have made our fortunes through the internet."

"Yes, I'm not going to sugar-coat it, you will be walking into complete chaos, of that I have no doubt," Tm said. "And I want to thank you all in advance for everything you are about to do."

"I only wish we had known sooner," Al said. "So let's get going. The others have already arrived, it is time for us to do our parts."

"I will return to the operations room, and I will give you a countdown to departure," Bk said. "Good luck." He clicked his fingers and disappeared, leaving the 9 of them sat in a circle, with nothing to do but wait. Tm wondered if they should have a strategy of sort, a sign they could give each other, so that they would know that their plans were working.

He voiced his thoughts out loud to the group.

"According to Bk, we were fairly cut off from the normal world, but quite influential. So perhaps a symbol could be used as a signal, or a particular word?" Fi mused. "Something that we could project into the world, to show that we are changing things?"

"It has to be unusual enough to stand out," Mo said. "But commonplace enough to be used in our products or businesses."

"Infinity," Tm said. "The word infinity, or the symbol." He smiled at the men. "In honour of where we found you. And in honour of Mg, whom Bk will keep in contact with, in case we need his help."

"It's perfect," Jr said. The other's nodded in agreement.

In Tm's ear at that moment, he heard Bk's voice.

"Are you ready?" Tm nodded, and saw the others nodding too.

"Good luck. Five, four, three, two, one..."

Tm saw the others disappear one by one, then as he heard the word 'one' he closed his eyes.

# AU

## CHAPTER TWENTY-EIGHT

Over two decades of tormenting humans on Earth hadn't softened Au's heart.

If anything, it had just made it harder, and darker. The onslaught of the last few years, of war, famine, droughts, and her piece de resistance - a global pandemic - had just shown her what she had known all along, even back when Mg had left their planet to come to this awful place. Humans didn't deserve to live. They didn't deserve all the luxuries they had, all the love, all the joy. They had sucked the light out of her home, and now she was relishing in doing it to theirs.

It had been a long journey, and there were times when she wondered if it was worth it, and whether she should just leave the humans to their misery, and go to another realm or dimension. But she was glad that she had persisted in her revenge.

Because it was about to get as sweet as it could possibly get.

It had taken a considerable amount of time, mainly due to the constraints of the technology available on Earth, but with the unwitting help of her fellow Zubenelgenubians,

Au had finally got her master plan together, and her initial tests were proving to be successful. Knowing how easily led humans were (the pandemic had proven that) Au had no doubt that they would fall for her latest plan. Because it had been created entirely under the guise of helping humans to live better lives. But by the time they realised how utterly miserable their lives were, it would be too late. Just as it was too late for them to live without the tech and she and her kin had created.

Sure, there were a few humans who had resisted, who had remained low tech, but they were generally older, and Au was confident that once they were out of the way, the take up would be high. And therefore her revenge would be complete.

"Aurelia? I have Bill on the phone for you?"

Au looked up at her assistant, and nodded. They were working out of a makeshift office in her apartment, mainly so they could stay low key and off the radar. She had lost touch with Tm long ago, and feared that he may be working against her. She had seen the look in his eyes, the last time she saw him, and knew that he was having doubts. So she kept changing names and locations, so that he couldn't find her and stop her.

She picked up the phone on her desk (she still had a landline) and hit the button. "Hi, Bill, what can I do for you?"

* * *

Later that afternoon, Au stared at her screenin joyful disbelief. This was it, the moment she had been working towards for the last few years. Just the tap of a single button would begin the complete unravelling of the human race. Well, what was left of it, anyway.

Desperate to share the moment with someone, she called out for her assistant to join her.

"What's wrong, Aurelia?" her assistant asked.

"Nothing," Au replied, "I'm about to finally complete the project, and I just wanted to share this moment with someone as I hit the button to complete." She saw the lacklustre enthusiasm on her admittedly overworked and underpaid assistant, and wished she hadn't called her in to witness this historic moment. She should have just relished it by herself. She waved her hand at her assistant.

"Never mind, go back to whatever you were doing, sorry to interrupt."

Her assistant nodded, and left the room, leaving the Starperson to revel in her own genius, her own wickedness. Au had deliberately kept her assistant in the dark as to the scope of the project, so she had no idea of the impact it was going to have. Or just how brilliant it was.

Au breathed in deeply, then reached out to tap the key that would set her whole masterplan into action.

But nothing happened.

Frowning, she hit the key again, but nothing changed. She refreshed the screen, and got an error page.

*Not connected to the internet.*

She opened up the Wi-Fi tab, and there was no connection.

Au sighed and picked up her cell phone, but saw that there was no connection there either.

Not bothering to yell this time, she went to the outer room and found her assistant frantically refreshing her screen.

"I have no connection," Au said, "You haven't either?"

"No, not on my phone, laptop, nothing. The service must be completely down. Did you manage to launch it?"

Au shook her head. "No, it went down just before I could. I hope it's not down for long. But seeing as it is for now, you might as well call it a day, there's not a whole lot we can do without a connection."

Her assistant nodded and gathered her things and put them in her bag. "It will be back by tomorrow, I can carry on with my tasks then. Take the night off, yeah? You've been working nonstop on this project. Celebrate! It's done, after all these years."

Au tried to smile, but she was feeling too frustrated at being stopped seconds from completion. "Sure, I'll do that."

She watched her assistant leave, then went back to her desk and spent the next two hours refreshing her screen and checking constantly for a connection. Finally, she gave up and went to her bedroom to sleep. Despite being in a human body, she found that she could get away with little food as long as she slept enough and stayed hydrated. She found human needs quite inconvenient. Hunger and tiredness had meant that it had taken longer than she had anticipated to do everything she had come to Earth to do.

But she was so close now.

As she slipped off her clothes and got under the covers, she closed her eyes and thought of the magical moment when she would finally complete her project, her mission. And the humans would finally get what was coming to them.

She couldn't wait.

# CHAPTER TWENTY-NINE

By the third day of no internet or cell signal, Au was completely losing her mind. She had fired her assistant, as she couldn't afford to keep paying her when there was no work that could be done, and she had taken to staying in bed to conserve her energy. Her food stocks were low and her cash was running out.

She hadn't planned to stay on Earth once she had hit the button and launched her magnum opus, so she had been running down her food supplies and hadn't bothered to keep much cash in the apartment. It seemed ridiculous that she had plenty of money, but was alone in an apartment with barely any food, just waiting for the internet to come back.

The day after the connection went, she had reached out to Bill and the other Zubenelgenubians to find out who had done it, because surely it had to be one of them. But they all swore that they had nothing to do with it, and they were scrabbling as much as she was. Though they were slightly more prepared for the apocalypse, with their bunkers, food reserves and cash. They had all invited her to stay with them, but she was sure that the outage wouldn't last long, that the connection would be restored and she could finally hit the damn button.

But now she wasn't so sure. She stared at her cell phone, mentally willing it to find some connection, anything. She had never felt so disconnected, not on Earth, anyway.

She slammed her phone down on the bedside table and let out a frustrated yell. She threw back the covers, got up, then pulled out random clothing from her drawers, before stomping to the bathroom to have a shower. She needed to get out of the apartment, and she needed to find some food. She glanced at the mirror and saw that her already thin frame was beginning to look skeletal. It would be an awful kind of karma if she starved to death before she finally took her revenge against the humans.

Once she was clean and dressed, she gathered the last of her change, and headed out the door for the first time in two days. Even though she had stayed at home far longer during the pandemic, she had always had constant connection to the outside world through her phone, and hadn't felt cut off in the same way she had for the previous seventy-two hours. She had also had food delivered to her door and a fridge full of supplies.

She set off down the street, blinking in the sunlight. A young couple passed her, and nodded and smiled, but she ignored them. She was too hungry and tired to pretend to be a nice human.

Au wasn't surprised to see signs of looting in the stores she passed, humans were vile, violent monsters, after all. There were boarded up broken windows, glass littering the sidewalk, graffiti on the walls, and a definite increase in police presence. She wondered if humans were even capable of remaining calm and logical in the face of crisis. Considering the extent of the damage, it seemed they were not.

She reached the convenience store on the corner, and went inside. She was glad to be in the cool of the air conditioning, and pleased that it appeared intact and operational. Though there were two very burly security guards at the door.

Au searched the aisles for her favourite snacks, noting that the majority of the shelves were empty. If there was one thing she could credit the humans for, it was inventing the tastiest snacks. She wasn't surprised that there was little stock left.

Au knew that the snacks were of little nutritional value, but she didn't care at that point, she just needed a sugar hit. She was beginning to feel a bit dizzy.

She grabbed some energy drinks, chips and candy bars and took her haul to the checkout, hoping that the pile of shrapnel in her pocket would be enough to cover it.

The old man behind the counter rang up her purchases, only raising his eyebrow slightly at her choices. She was glad he didn't say anything out loud, she wasn't in the mood for his judgement.

"That will be twelve dollars and ninety-eight cents," he said, putting everything in a thin plastic bag.

Au pulled all of the change out of her pocket and quickly counted it, realising she was a dollar fifty short. "Um," she said placing the change on the counter. "I'll leave one of the drinks? Sorry, I ran out of cash and can't access my accounts at the moment."

"You and the rest of the world," the man in line behind her chuckled.

Au turned to snap at him, when she saw him reach his hand out to add a dollar fifty to her cash on the counter. She frowned at him. "Why would you do that? Don't you need it?"

The man glanced her up and down and smiled. "I think you need it more? Though it wouldn't hurt to get some real food too, when did you last eat properly? There are food banks running for those who haven't been able to get into their accounts. And if you speak to the banks, they have set up a program to allow people to take money out. You don't need to suffer."

Au felt tears forming in her eyes, and a rush of emotion that she was unused to feeling. "Um, thank you, I didn't know that."

The old man behind the counter held her bag out to her, and she took it, wiping her tears away with the back of her hand. "Thank you," she said to the man who had paid for her food. "How can I repay you?" If there was one thing Au hated, it was feeling indebted.

The man shook his head, and placed his groceries on the counter. "No need, just pay it forwards when you can, and get some proper food, yeah?"

Au nodded, feeling more tears welling up at his kindness. She turned away and left the store before she could embarrass herself further. She wasn't sure why she was feeling so emotional suddenly. *It must be because of the lack of food*, she reasoned.

Outside, the heat of the midday sun hit her and she reached into her bag for the cold energy drink. She twisted the cap off and slugged down nearly half the bottle in one go.

She set off down the street. Feeling re-energised and still

slightly embarrassed, she kept walking until she reached the shore. She saw few civilians but many armed soldiers and  police officers. Those who were out appeared to be wandering aimlessly, unsure what to do.

Au could smell the salty ocean air and hear the waves before she could see the sparkling blue Pacific Ocean. Feeling a bit overheated by then, she found a bench under the shade of a palm tree and sat down, pulling out her favourite corn chips from her bag and munching on them while watching two surfers in the waves.

"Can you spare some change?"

Au shaded her eyes with her hand and looked up to see a woman with a shopping cart, wearing nothing but a dirty t-shirt and shorts, her bare feet dirty and covered in cuts.

Au shook her head, and the woman nodded in disappointment then turned to leave. "Wait, I don't have change, but I have some chips and a soda." Au pulled them out of the bag and held them up, even though her mind was screaming - *This is all you have! What are you doing?*

The woman smiled, and Au noticed she was missing a few teeth. "Thank you, may I sit?"

Au nodded and the woman sat on the bench next to her and tore into the bag, eating handfuls of the chips like she had hadn't eaten in days, which she might not have.

"Are the soup kitchens not running?" Au asked, though still wondering why she cared.

The woman munched on the chips and shook her head. She chased them down with some soda. "They ran out of food, and the banks are being shady on funding them."

"Wow, it's only been three days," Au said, thinking that perhaps the internet shutdown was actually the best kind of revenge. The humans seemed to have lost all ability to function normally. But it was not her revenge. Who else would have such a grudge against the humans? Because surely it was deliberate? Au couldn't imagine that the loss of the internet and cell networks on a global scale could have been a mere accident.

"Other than there not being any food, I think it's been kinda nice," the woman said as she finished the pack of chips in record speed.

"Nice?" Au repeated, wondering how this woman, who clearly had nothing, could find a silver lining in the current situation.

"Yeah, I've talked to more folk in the last three days than the last three years out on the streets. Usually people don't look up from their phones, don't even notice me."

"How did you end up on the streets?" Au asked, curious in spite of herself.

"Pandemic," the woman said. "Got ill, couldn't pay the medical bills, lost my job, and everyone was struggling you know? Couldn't stay with friends, got no family, so here I am." The woman shrugged, and Au felt tears prickling again. Why was she feeling emotional? Wasn't this what she wanted? To cause the most suffering she could? To teach the humans a lesson?

But what lesson was she teaching this woman? How to survive with nothing? How to see the silver linings in the direst of circumstances? For what? This woman had no idea that the planet Zubenelgenubi was dead. That the humans had caused it to die with their selfishness. She was too busy suffering, trying to find her next meal, to even consider the bigger picture.

"How did you keep going?" Au asked. She had only managed three days on less food than normal. Three years sounded impossible.

"Things got pretty dark, especially early on, when I was still recovering. I had no bed, no clean water, no food. But then I met Jan."

Au looked at the woman after a moment of silence. "Jan?"

The woman smiled. "Yeah Jan was in the same boat as me, except she was never going to recover. She died a couple months after we met."

"I'm so sorry," Au said automatically, even though she wasn't sure if she really was. But she was curious as to how Jan's death had made things any easier.

"It was sad, but meeting Jan, spending time with her, the two of us with nothing and no one; made me realise that in this world, in this life, all you really need is to be seen. To have your life witnessed by another. To know that someone cares that you are alive, and is sad if you die. And Jan cared about me, I cared about her." The woman shrugged. "Whenever possible, I try to show people that I care. And that they matter."

Au drank the rest of her energy drink, and threw the bottle in the litter can next to her while contemplating the woman's words. "I'm glad you had Jan," she said, thinking about her own lonely time in the dark, missing everyone she loved. Had that been all she needed? For someone to show that they cared?

The woman stood up and threw away the empty chip packet. She tucked the half-drunk bottle of soda in her shopping cart. "Thank you for the snack, and the conversation. I hope you have a great day." She walked a few steps then stopped and looked back at Au. "And remember, no matter how dark it gets, there is always a little light somewhere. You just have to find it."

Au nodded, her mind whirring too much to form a response. She watched the woman trudge away, pushing her cart along the hot sidewalk. Surely her feet were getting burnt?

Before she could fully think it through, Au reached down and undid her laces, slipped off her shoes and ran after the woman.

*　*　*

Au arrived back at her apartment a short while later, and was sitting on the floor of her dingy lounge that had no sofa, just a makeshift desk her assistant had worked for years, and boxes of papers related to her project stacked haphazardly everywhere. She had a glass of water in her hand, her socks were filthy from the walk home, and her mind was still whirling. She couldn't stop thinking about the barefoot homeless woman, and the kind man at the convenience store. She should have tried to visit the local food bank, or even her own bank to see if she could get some money, but she couldn't think straight. Also, she had other resources, she could just call Bill or Mark, and they would get food to her immediately. But she was too proud to ask them for help. After all, she was the genius mastermind here. Wasn't she?

She didn't need anyone else to help her, did she?

The tears were falling before she could fully form the thoughts, but she realised as they soaked the front of her shirt that she was just truly, deeply, lonely.

Interactions with two complete strangers had reduced her to an emotional wreck, because she realised that in her bid to destroy the humans, what she had actually desperately needed was their love, warmth and connection.

When was the last time she'd had any human physical contact? A hug, a kiss, a touch? She honestly couldn't remember. In fact, she wasn't sure that she had experienced any at all in her current incarnation. Initially, it was because she wasn't used to having a physical body, but aside from the odd handshake, she had resisted any kind of touch because she didn't want to connect with humans, she didn't want to feel empathy for them. They were the enemy, after all.

But were they? Had they really killed her planet? Or had the planet died simply because her kin all wanted to help others? Wanted to experience human lives? Had the humans really stolen the light, or had the light left of its own accord?

Au had to admit that the smell of the ocean, the feeling of the sun on her skin, and the salty taste of corn chips was almost worth losing her home planet for. She had been squelching the joy and satisfaction that small, simple things brought her. How alive she felt when she had dipped her toes into the waves for the very first time. How much she loved the taste of ice cream. How sweet the scent of the roses that grew in front of her apartment building were.

Did humans deserve such wonders? Did they deserve such a beautiful planet when they were hell-bent on destroying it?

She sighed and sipped the water that she had forgotten she was still holding. Were they hell-bent on destroying it though, or was that just her?

Feeling like she was completely losing her mind, she got up and went to her bedroom, and picked up her cell phone. There was still no network. She put it down and went to the tiny room she used as an office and sat at her desk. Who could she call? She had no friends. She had lost touch with Tm long ago, otherwise he would have been the one she would have reached out to. Even though she was still sure that he was working against her. She sighed. He was probably right to.

Au picked up the landline phone and listened to the dial tone for a few moments before hanging up. She would wait another day to see if the internet was restored, then she would reach out to one of the Zubenelgenubians.

If she was still alive by then.

# CHAPTER THIRTY

"Aurelia? Are you in there?"

Au blinked, but her eyes were so dry from dehydration that her eyelids were sticking together. She sat up and rubbed her eyes. "Hello?" she called out, her mouth dry, her voice barely a croak.

The light switched on in the dark room and Au groaned at the sudden brightness. She squinted at the figure in the doorway. "Jenni?" she said, confused. What was her assistant doing in her bedroom?

"Jeez, Aurelia, when was the last time you ate anything? Where have you been? I tried your house phone, but you didn't answer."

Au frowned, trying to get her parched brain to form thoughts. "I've been here? What are you doing here? I fired you?"

Jenni sighed. "You fired me from my job, but that doesn't stop me caring about you. I thought you of all people would have been prepared. Did you have no food stocked up? No cash? Ever since the pandemic I've been telling you to keep your cupboards full."

Au shook her head. "I just hadn't been shopping for a while, I was too busy with my project."

Jenni sighed. "Well I reminded you several times. Nevermind, get a shower, get dressed, you're coming with me."

"Um, where are we going?" Au asked.

"To get some food. You were skinny before, but now you just look like you haven't eaten in a month, even though it's only been six days. We need to get some calories into you." She picked up an empty chip packet off the bedside table with disdain. "And not just empty calories. You have ten minutes, come on."

Au wanted to resist, but she was too tired and light-headed to form much of an argument, so she did as she was told, all the while wondering why her quiet assistant who had shown zero interest in her health and wellbeing before was suddenly coming to save her?

She washed and dressed slowly, taking far more than the allotted ten minutes, as her sense of balance was off and she kept having to hold onto the wall.

When she finally came out of the bedroom into the lounge, she found Jenni sat at her desk, tapping away at her laptop.

"What are you doing?" she asked, slipping her shoes on. She felt a tiny pang of regret that she'd given her favourite shoes away, but she figured she could get another pair.

"Just checking my email, not that I expect there to be any, after all, who would have sent any? No one had connection."

Au frowned. "Wait, what? How can you check your email?"

Jenni closed her laptop and slipped it back in her bag.

"What do you mean? The internet came back yesterday morning. Sometime in the early hours. That's why I stopped by. I thought you might have messaged to say you'd finally launched your project. When you didn't, I got worried." Jenni took in the shock on Au's face and smiled. "Though I'm guessing by your face that you didn't know? Didn't your phone start pinging? That's how I knew."

Au went back to her room and picked up her phone, which she had stopped looking at more than two days before. It was completely dead. She plugged it in, then went back to the lounge. "Phone was dead. Wow. It's been back for almost two days and I didn't even realise?"

Jenni shrugged. "I guess we all got used to not having it. I've read so many books over the last few days, and walked miles, and seen friends I hadn't seen for years."

Au looked at her assistant and realised that she did look like she was glowing with health. What a contrast with her own starved, neglected body.

"Did you want to launch the project before we eat?" Jenni waved her hand towards the tiny box room where Au's computer was.

Au shook her head. "No, let's go get some food. I'm guessing our credit cards work now? In which case, it's my treat."

Jenni laughed. "Yes, they do. But it's my treat. I insist." She went to Au's front door and Au followed her out of the apartment and into the evening sun.

* * *

"Are you sure you're okay?" Jenni asked for the fifth time.

Au realised that she was playing with the food on her

plate rather than eating it, and set her fork down with a sigh. "I'm sorry, I think my stomach has shrunk."

"Yes, to the size of a pea I reckon, you've only had a couple of mouthfuls." Jenni set her own fork down too and dabbed her mouth with her napkin. "I just feel awful, I should have checked on you sooner, but well, when you fired me, you didn't sound like you wanted to see me again."

Au tilted her head to one side and stared at her assistant for a moment. "So why did you come back?"

Jenni shrugged. "I don't know really, I just woke up this morning, and knew that I had to come and see you. It just wasn't even an option or a question, I had to." She picked up her fork and began eating again. "And I also wondered if you had launched your project yet. I never really did understand it, exactly, but it seemed pretty cool."

Au resumed eating as well, mainly to avoid speaking. She had done nothing over the last three days other than think about her project. And about the man in the store. And the homeless woman she gave her shoes to.

Her desire for revenge had burnt out. Finally, after all these eons, she no longer wished to harm humans. And the sudden lack of rage, after all the time and energy she had spent on executing the perfect retaliation against the humans, was perplexing, and quite frankly, frustrating.

Because not only did she have no desire to launch her project anymore, she also wanted to try and reverse some of the damage she had already caused. She had no idea how she would do that, but she knew she had to try. Perhaps if she had spent even a little bit of time around humans before now, she might have calmed down sooner. But she had avoided human contact as much as possible, hiding behind a screen all these years on Earth, seeking out the very worst of humanity to prove her right. That the humans didn't deserve to be shown any compassion. That they were destroyers, they were killers. They were evil.

Au managed to eat some more of her food and looked up at Jenni, who was watching her with concern.

"You look a little bit brighter," Jenni commented, refilling her water glass from the jug on the table.

Au shrugged. "I feel a bit better for eating. Thank you for forcing me to come out."

Jenni smiled. "Of course. I'm just so glad that the darkness didn't consume you completely."

Au's eyes widened and she frowned at her former assistant. She stared at her features, staring into her eyes, noticing for the first time a lighter ring of colour around her pupils. A shock of recognition jolted through her body.

"Jr?" she whispered.

Jenni's smile grew wider. "So you do remember, Au."

Au's mouth dropped open. "But we've been working together for years, how did I not know?"

"Because Jenni didn't know, not consciously. I was in another realm when I heard what was happening, and I returned to the Academy to assist, before choosing to return to Earth because I hoped I could help." She smiled at Au. "Imagine my surprise when I realised that the rogue alien everyone was searching for was in fact my old boss?" She shook her head. "I always felt awful for leaving you in the darkness, all those eons ago. I should never have left you alone for so long. Perhaps that's what drew our souls together."

Au was speechless. Her disinterested assistant was really the pilot from her home planet? The last being she had communicated with before being consumed by the darkness? It seemed so improbable, but at the same time, completely perfect.

"You don't want me to launch my project, do you? You came back to stop me."

"Will it cause more destruction and suffering?" Jenni asked gently.

"That was the general idea, yes," Au replied sarcastically.

"Do you still want to launch it? You didn't seem too keen to do it before we left this evening."

Au was quiet for a moment, and for the first time since they had sat down to eat in the restaurant, she became aware of the people around them, each having their own conversations over their meals. There were couples celebrating, there were others having quiet arguments. There was laughter and teasing and general merriment. No one was staring at a screen, they all appeared to be in the present moment, living their lives, completely unaware that amongst them was an alien who had hoped to cause them all to suffer.

She frowned when a thought occurred to her. "Wait, was it you who took down the internet? To stop me?"

Jenni laughed. "Goodness no, I don't have that kind of power."

"Then who did?"

Jenni looked like she was debating with herself, probably trying to work out how much to tell Au. After all, she could use the information against her, and still wreak more destruction. But eventually, she appeared to decide to be honest and open about what she knew.

"It was Bk. At the Academy. He was trying to re-initiate the walk-in program, and the only way to do that was to reboot the internet. He hadn't intended for it to be down for so long, he was worried about the effects, but from what I've seen so far, it seems like the humans adapted fairly well." She raised an eyebrow. "Well, mostly."

Au knew she meant her, not eating and taking care of herself. Or perhaps she meant the looting and police presence. Au wasn't sure.

"What I don't understand is why you didn't go to Bill's, or Mark's. Surely they invited you?"

Au nodded. "They did, I just didn't think it would go on this long, and well, I didn't want their help."

"Just like you refused mine," Jenni said softly. "I don't know why you keep punishing yourself, by isolating and starving yourself. Whatever made you think you deserved that?"

Au's eyes filled with tears, but she made no move to wipe them away. She tried to smile at her kin but failed. "Because he left me, Jr. Mg left me on that planet to fade away, and I have never recovered from that." Her tears fell one by one. "And then Tm left. He was not my Flame, but we were so close, and after that, I felt like I had nothing left to shine for."

Jenni reached across the table and took Au's hand in hers. It was the first human touch Au had experienced in years, and it almost gave her an electric shock. "They left because they wanted to save you, because they wanted to make sure that you lived, that the planet lived. They didn't leave because you didn't deserve to be loved."

Au gripped Jenni's hand in return. "If that was the case, when the Diamond Age ended, why didn't they come back to me?"

Jenni frowned but didn't speak. Because like Au, she had no idea what the answer was.

# CHAPTER THIRTY-ONE

"I trust by now that you have all had a chance to see what destruction we have caused on Earth over the last twenty-three years."

"Um, don't you mean the destruction *you* have made us cause?" Mo corrected gently.

Au sighed, but nodded. "You are right, the destruction that I have caused, through you." She looked around at the seven Zubenelgenubians, in their human forms that she had got to know so well over the last two decades, but now glowing with the auras of their conscious souls. She could feel the disappointment radiating from them, but having Jr sat beside her gave her the strength to continue. "There is little point in trying to justify my actions or even apologise for them, as that will not help the humans, or repair the damage. What is needed now, is to restore peace, health and love to the planet."

"You may think explanations are unnecessary," Al interjected, "but why have you suddenly changed your mind? Changed your course? How can we trust that this is not all just a ruse? Just a way to get us to create yet more chaos and darkness?”

Au paused for a moment. He was right, of course, they needed to know that she was genuine, that her intentions really were to help, and not harm. But how to explain her complete change of heart?

“A very long time ago, a friend tried to help me. She tried to bring me into the light, but I had been alone for so long, I didn’t think I deserved her help.” Au caught Jr’s eye, who smiled at her encouragingly. “Then just a few days ago, I needed help. But I couldn’t bring myself to ask anyone I knew to help me. But out of nowhere, a complete stranger stepped up, and helped me out. And then someone reached out to me for help, and I offered what I could. Then when that same friend from so long ago, came back and offered me a hand, I took it.” She took a deep breath, looking at each man in turn. “These simple interactions made me realise that no one can exist in isolation. No one can thrive or even survive without the give and take of help and love, and support and friendship. And that I only felt bitter towards the humans because they had everything I wanted, everything I needed, and yet they didn’t appear to appreciate it at all. Instead, they were destroying their own planet and the universe, in their greediness for more. But they don’t deserve to suffer any further because of my bitterness and jealousy. They deserve a chance.” She took another deep breath. “Just as I hope you think I deserve a chance too, to earn your trust and prove that I can be a bright light again, not a shadow of pain and suffering.”

The room was silent for a while after her speech, and after a few moments, Au sat down, and awaited their thoughts. Jr patted her on the knee and Au nodded to her friend in appreciation of her support.

Si was the first to speak. "We can feel your sincerity, though I still have some reservations. How do you propose we fix everything? All we have is our technology, and money, which as we know, cannot fix all the ills of the world."

"Perhaps not," Au agreed. "But it can make a good start. I propose that instead of seemingly competing with each other, all eight of us join together to create tech that will bring humanity together as one, and finally erase the hunger, war, and pain that is currently present."

"That is a lofty goal," Fi said. "Do you have any idea how that might be possible?"

Au shook her head, "Not yet, but we are some of the brightest minds in the universe, I am sure we can think of something.

"I have an idea," Jr said with a smile.

*   *   *

"Are you sure you don't want to stay? See what you have helped create?"

Au smiled at Jr and shook her head. "The others have everything they need now, everything is in motion. I'm not needed here, I should never have been here. It is time for me to go home."

Jr frowned. "Back to Zubenelgenubi? Back to the darkness? But why? You have atoned for your actions, you have worked so hard for these last few months to make things right, why punish yourself by isolating yourself once again?"

Au hugged her oldest friend. "I will return to the Academy, and I will allow them to decide my fate. If they think I should go back to my planet, then I will. But if there is somewhere else I can be of service, either in this galaxy or another, I will go wherever I am needed. I understand now, that we are created to serve others. That happiness can only be found in the giving and receiving of love and support."

Jr squeezed Au's hand and smiled. "As long as you know that there is no need to punish yourself further. That there are those who love you, deeply. Even Mg and Tm."

Au shrugged. "Maybe one day I will see them again, and I will understand why they did not return to me. But even if I don't, I do understand that what they did, they did with loving intentions."

Jr looked around Au's empty apartment. "You are leaving tonight?"

"Yes, everything is in order. I just wanted to give you this." Au held out a cheque.

Jr took it and saw the amount. Her eyes widened and she gasped. "What is this?"

"It is what I should have paid you, all these years. And I will have no use for it, so I want you to have it, and to start that business you always dreamed of."

Jr looked at her, her eyes sparkling with tears. "Thank you, Au. I promise I will do just that."

"Good. Now, shall we have one last coffee? And get some snacks? I'm really going to miss human food."

Jr wiped away her tears and put the cheque carefully in her pocket. "You do know that the snacks you love the most aren't really food, right? Just engineered chemicals that taste good?"

"Absolutely, let's go get some."

Jr laughed and led the way out of the apartment. Au switched off the lights and followed her out, looking forward to one final human experience before begining her journey home.

*　*　*

"Welcome back, Au."

Au looked up at Gold's kind, wrinkled face, but then quickly looked down at the mists below them. "Am I really welcome? I should think you would very much like to damn me for all eternity?"

Gold reached out and placed his hand on her shoulder. "You should know by now that I do not condemn, nor punish. And that you have already done that to yourself."

Au sighed and looked back up at his face, and saw his gentle, non-judgemental smile. "I hope that I have done enough to reverse some of the damage. That the others will be able to steer the Earth in a better direction. And that perhaps, one day, I may be forgiven."

Gold chuckled. "My dear, Au. The only forgiveness you require is your own. There is no one here nor on Earth who holds a grudge against you."

Au frowned. "Well they should. My actions were unforgivable."

"You were alone for a very long time. It is entirely understandable. And we also all played our parts in the recent chaos. You weren't the only one who made bad decisions."

Au frowned. "You consider yourself to be one of them?"

Gold nodded. "I lost the one I loved because I made the wrong choices. I went to Earth with the others to help with the shift, but once all was under control I came back here to the mists, where I will remain for eternity, atoning for my choices."

"I guess none of us are immune to jealousy, loss or atonement."

Gold's smile deepened. "Indeed. We may be from other planets and realms, but we are all mostly human underneath it all."

Not long before, the idea of being human would have made Au shudder in disgust. But now, she understood completely. In surrendering to the darkness, and allowing it to take over her innate light, she had become very human indeed.

"Where would you have me spend eternity in atonement? Can I be of service here? Or in another realm?"

Gold shook his head, and Au's light dimmed. "I think it may be time for you to return home," he said.

"To my own planet?" Though she had expected he might say that, she felt deflated all the same. But perhaps another few eons in the dark to think about her awful behaviour was what she deserved.

Gold nodded. "Your ship awaits, outside the Academy. Safe travels."

Au bowed slightly to the Elder and walked through the mists past him, towards the Earth Angel Training Academy, where her ship awaited to take her home.

* * *

Her journey home through the galaxy was relatively uneventful, with just the odd meteor shower and near miss with space junk. The ship had been updated and modified by Bk, and needed very little tending to, leaving Au to her thoughts. She had crossed paths with Bk when she arrived at the Academy, and despite doing her best to apologise to him for her wrongdoings, he wouldn't hear of it, and kept cutting her off, insisting that all had ended well. But she could see in his energy that the stress had taken its toll. She tried to apologise for trapping him and the others in the same day for over twenty years also, but he wouldn't let her do that, either. He really was a very bright, kind soul, and she wished there was something she could do for him to make up for all the stress and struggle she had caused. Perhaps there would be, one day.

He had echoed Gold's words, that no one was infallible, and beyond making bad decisions. But Au felt that she had made many more than most, and that she deserved this exile to her dead home planet.

Lulled by the billions of stars shooting past her ship as she sped through the galaxy, Au's thoughts eventually quieted and she reached a feeling of peace, surrender and even forgiveness. After all, if she didn't forgive herself, wouldn't she just become bitter again after several more eons in the darkness?

By the time she was within range of her planet, Au was ready to resume her existence in the darkness, this time, peacefully. But as she approached what her screens were telling her was her beloved Zubenelgenubi, she was confused to see that the planet she was approaching was lit up like a beacon. She scanned the screens and tapped on the navigation system, to make sure it was correctly calibrated, but the information all relayed that the shining planet before her was indeed her home.

Had she still been in her human form, she would have certainly been crying at this moment. Tears of sheer awe and joy. Instead, she could feel herself glowing brighter, and by the time her ship docked itself at the station, she was glimmering brighter than she ever had before.

She exited the craft, and had only moved just beyond it when she was greeted with the most beautiful and unbelievable sight.

"Mg?" she communicated, still feeling in complete shock and awe. "Is that you?"

The light being moved towards her and their light merged, and a waterfall of words, emotions and feelings tumbled back and forth between them, as they reconnected after such a long separation.

"Where have you been, my love?" she asked him, feeling so very happy to have reunited, but still needing to know why it had taken him so long to return.

"I was in infinity, with the others, we were tasked to experience it, so that we could potentially create more harmonious worlds. When Tm and Jr came to find us, and took the seven back to Earth, they asked me to remain there, in case it was of use."

"Infinity came from you? Jr's idea and all the new tech? You sent it?"

Mg glowed brightly. "Yes, I was able to communicate what they needed to create the new world. And when it seemed my mission there was done, I knew I needed to bring that knowledge home, to Zubenelgenubi, to regenerate it."

Au took in more of her surroundings, and saw the many light beings there, and the light of the planet as a whole. "It's incredible! So you weren't punishing me by staying away?"

Mg's light dimmed slightly, causing Au to merge with him further, to lighten his energy. "That was never my intent, ever. In all honesty, I had no idea of the time that had passed. After all, infinity is quite timeless. But as soon as I heard word of the demise of Zubenelgenubi, I knew I had to return."

"And you did all this?" Au asked, in awe.

"No, when I returned, the planet had already begun to regenerate, and many Zubenelgenubians had returned. Together, we have made it a brighter, stronger planet. As you will see."

"So Gold wasn't exiling me, after all," Au mused.

"Not at all. You have atoned for your actions, my love. And between us, we have done all we can for the humans. Now it is time for you to live in the light, with me."

Au's light blended with Mg's, as they embraced for what seemed like a blissful eternity.

"Welcome home, my love," Mg communicated. "Let's begin our new chapter."

The very last of the bitterness, darkness and sadness in Au dissolved, and she and Mg moved as one towards their new home, and their future which stretched out infinitely before them, shining brightly.

# VELVET

## CHAPTER THIRTY-TWO

It was six months since Velvet had arrived back on Earth, and it was nearly Christmas. In that very short space of time, life had changed entirely on planet Earth for her and everyone else on it.

Once the Earth Angels all returned, and then the seven and Jr, they all quickly got to work and turned things around. The most surprising thing, was that Au had a complete change of heart, and helped them to create Infinity. It was a whole other level to the internet, in that it connected humans on mental, emotional and spiritual levels. This allowed them to truly see themselves in others, to truly empathise and connect, and to make sure that every single human on the planet was housed, clothed, fed and loved.

The project, once launched, had the most incredible ripple effect. Wars were resolved, aid and food and support distributed to those in need, people abandoned their devices and screens in favour of communicating with those around them, their families, friends, neighbours. So many illnesses and diseases were healed simply by people not feeling isolated and lonely anymore.

Velvet felt as though her part in it all had been minimal, though Aria and Amethyst and her other Earth Angel friends had assured her that she was the reason that they had all returned. Which had set things in motion to stop Au from destroying the planet completely.

But still, as she tried to get on with a normal human life, Velvet found herself longing for home, for Laguz, and their lives together in the Seventh Dimension.

Gold had explained that Laguz had been ready to come with them, but the Elder had requested that the Atlantean remain at the Academy to assist Bk. Velvet felt that was simply an excuse, and that it was really because Gold hadn't wanted her to be distracted by her Flame's presence.

Now that peace had been restored, and humanity was healing and on track for something resembling the Diamond Age again, she assumed Laguz would come to Earth as a walk-in and join her.

But six months later, she was still alone. And doing very mundane things, like washing her clothes and cleaning her flat.

Her phone vibrating pulled her out of her melancholic musings and she hit the accept button when she saw her friend's name.

"Magenta! How's it going? Are you well? Yuletide greetings." Velvet put the call on speakerphone while she continued to fold her clothes.

"Velvet! Yes, all is well. Happy Yuletide! Are you busy?"

Velvet raised an eyebrow at the pile of clean clothes and laughed. "No, not really, just a boring Saturday, washing clothes. You?"

"I'm in the car, on my way to yours, pack some stuff,

we're going away for the week."

Velvet paused mid-fold. "What? Where? I'm working this week, not sure I can get out of it at such short notice?"

"Say you're ill! You never take time off! And it's Christmas! Surely the office closes down for a few days? I'll be there in thirty minutes! Pack a raincoat and lots of jumpers, I think it might be a bit breezy when we get there!"

The call cut off before Velvet could reply. She stood in her bedroom for a moment, wondering what she should do. But then she remembered that Magenta was a powerful Seer. If she thought Velvet needed to go away with her for the week, then that was exactly what she needed to do. It also seemed like a much better way to spend Christmas than to stay in her flat alone, and going to work.

She grabbed a bag from the wardrobe and started shoving in the clean clothes she had just folded, along with a couple of extra jumpers and a coat. It had been a very mild winter so far, so she wondered where they were going. Hopefully somewhere near the sea, she hadn't been to the coast in way too long.

As promised, half an hour later, Magenta was at her door, and Velvet was all packed and ready to go. She opened the door to her friend and they hugged. "So good to see you, Old Soul! This is a surprise, what brought on this sudden need for a trip?"

Magenta laughed and tapped the side of her forehead. "Oh come on, Velvet. You already know the answer to that!"

She took Velvet's bag from her and they went out to the car, where Beryl and Aria were waiting.

"Girl's trip!" Velvet exclaimed, thrilled to see her friends again. "Seriously, where are we going?" she asked as she got in and buckled up.

"It's a surprise!" Aria said excitedly. "And I've promised not to spoil it!"

Velvet chuckled. "Okay, well, I'm game! Let's go."

*   *   *

It was dark when they arrived at the B&B, and the four women were tired from sitting in the car for nearly six hours. To Velvet's delight, they had headed due South and ended up on the coast of Cornwall, and were staying in a small cottage, right by the sea. As they walked to the front door, the wind whipped around them, making Velvet shiver slightly, but the sound of the waves roaring in the darkness made her heart feel so much lighter.

It reminded her of home.

They found the key and went inside, grateful to discover that the owner had already lit a fire for them, and it was lovely and cosy inside. Aria made a beeline for the fire, warming herself by it. Beryl went to the kitchen to make them all tea, and Magenta went to check out the bedrooms. Velvet stood by the window, trying to peer out into the darkness, but mostly just saw the reflection of the room behind her. She couldn't wait to get outside and walk along the beach the next day.

"So are you guys really not going to tell me why we are here?" she asked. She had also asked during the car ride, but they had all changed the subject each time, or turned the music up louder.

"Magenta had a vision!" Aria squeaked. She clapped a hand over her mouth and immediately looked guilty. "Oops! Sorry, I know I wasn't supposed to say!"

"A vision? Magenta!" Velvet called up the stone stairs.

"What did you See?"

She could hear her friend chuckling as she re-joined them in the lounge. Beryl brought in a tray with four mismatched floral mugs on it.

The four of them sat and took a mug each, and Magenta smiled at Velvet. "This. I Saw us, here, the four of us. Drinking tea."

Velvet raised an eyebrow. "So you urgently found the cottage, booked it for Christmas and then kidnapped us all to create this scene?"

Aria giggled, and Beryl smiled. "I wouldn't say she kidnapped us, exactly," the Angel said.

"It felt important," Magenta said. She shrugged. "I have no idea why though! It was quite infuriating, and I had considered ignoring it, but it was so vivid. And it happened three times, so I figured I should listen, and so here we are."

"Really?" Velvet persisted. "This is the whole vision?"

Magenta nodded, and Velvet could see the truth in the Old Soul's eyes.

"Huh, okay, well, I have to say, it is a much better way to spend the Christmas week, so cheers, Earth Angels. Here's to fulfilling weird visions with no reasons why!"

Giggling, they all clinked their mugs together.

"Aren't your partners slightly annoyed though?" Velvet wondered. "Tim? Ben? Steve?"

"They understand that you guys come first," Beryl said.

"And Tim has gone home again," Aria said softly.

"What?" Velvet said, shocked. "Oh, Faerie, why didn't you say so? When did he leave?"

Aria shrugged. "A couple of weeks ago. He was missing his Flame, and I said he should go, he had been away from her for too long. I completely understand, I miss Linen so much. But I know he's at home waiting for me, and I know that this human life will zip by, so I can wait. I kinda want to see how things pan out, and how it differs to the Diamond Age."

"Oh, Faerie, that's still hard, I'm so sorry. You should have called me, this is meant to be the age of connection, of love and support."

"I had support," Aria said, smiling at Beryl. "Amethyst has been there for me too. I'm okay, I'm just glad that Tim gets to be happy now. He already spent an extra twenty years on Earth, he's done his time."

The women laughed at her words. "Being human does feel like a prison sentence at times," Beryl agreed.

"Let's hope we get let out early for good behaviour," Velvet said dryly. She was joking, but only slightly. Six months of waiting and hoping her Flame would come to find her meant that she had spent a considerable amount of time thinking about going home. Despite the infinite possibilities that surrounded her in this new world, she longed for her Flame's touch more.

"You know what, screw the tea," Magenta said suddenly. "Who fancies some mulled wine?"

There was a chorus of agreement, so the Old Soul got up to put some wine on the stove.

Velvet followed her out to the kitchen, and rinsed her empty mug out in the sink.

"Was this part of the vision too?" she teased gently.

Magenta chuckled. "No, but it *is* the Winter Solstice, and it's nearly Christmas. I think a little bit of mulled wine is called for, don't you?"

"Absolutely."

# CHAPTER THIRTY-THREE

Despite feeling slightly fuzzy-headed when she woke up, after their 'little bit of mulled wine' turned into a few bottles of red the night before, Velvet was glad to be up early and walking along the sand with Magenta the next morning.

"This brings back so many otherworldly memories," Magenta said, shivering in the chilly sea breeze. "Though it was never this cold on the other side."

Velvet laughed, and stopped to slip off her shoes that were already filled with gritty sand. She slipped off her socks as well and shoved them inside her shoes, then she went closer to the water's edge and let the waves wash over her feet.

"Wow!" she gasped, dancing backwards quickly. "The water wasn't so freezing either! That is very refreshing."

Magenta laughed. "I shall be keeping my shoes on, I'm afraid."

"I hear that cold water is good for your health," Velvet teased.

"I don't care what they say, I am not going in," Magenta said, moving a few paces further away from the water.

"Okay, okay," Velvet said, re-joining her friend as they made their way along the shore.

Suddenly, Magenta stopped and turned to face Velvet. Her gaze shifted to over her left shoulder, and Velvet knew that her friend was having a vision, so she waited patiently, while so many memories of this exact moment happening so long ago, washed over her.

When Magenta's gaze refocused on Velvet's face, she whispered to her friend, "What is it, Magenta? What did you See?"

Magenta's face lit up with a huge smile. "All of your dreams coming true," she said softly.

"My dreams?" Velvet asked curiously. "What do you mean?"

"Listen," Magenta said.

Velvet frowned and listened, but all she could hear was the roar of the waves behind her, and a gull calling in the distance. She shook her head. "To what?"

"Listen harder," Magenta insisted.

Velvet heeded her old friend and closed her eyes. She breathed slowly and deeply, and listened as hard as she could, and just when she was about to whisper that she still didn't understand, she heard it, faint, but clear.

Her eyes snapped open. "I can hear a piano," she said. She looked around them, up and down the shore. But unlike the vision she'd had so very long ago, it was not coming from the sea. Memories of long, tangled blond hair, green eyes and a shining fin flashed through her mind.

She looked up towards the dunes and saw a small cottage tucked just beyond it. "Do you think it's possible?" she whispered.

Magenta reached out and squeezed her hand. "I think

anything is possible. Go and find out."

Her breaths coming more quickly now, Velvet left her friend at the water's edge and made her way up the beach, over to the dunes, towards the cottage. She was oblivious to the grittiness of the sand between her toes, and the sea breeze tangling her long hair as the strains of the piano notes became clearer, and she could hear the familiar sonata calling to her.

Tears were rolling down her cheeks, and by the time she reached the back door of the cottage, and dropped her shoes on the doormat, she was a mess. She pulled a tissue out of her pocket and wiped her nose, drying her eyes on her sleeve. She wiped her bare feet on the mat, then took a deep breath and decided to knock. After all, the cottage could still just belong to a random stranger. But the door was ajar, so she pushed it open further, and the song became louder.

Holding her breath in excitement, anticipation and fear, she tiptoed barefoot into the house, feeling both like an intruder, and like someone who had finally come home after a very long trip away at sea. In the front room overlooking the beach, she finally found the source of the music.

Unable to make a sound, she breathed shallowly and watched the back of his blonde head until he played the very last note, and while it still hung in the air, she breathed his name.

"Laguz."

He went still then, his hands still hovering above the keys. Slowly, he turned around, and smiled at her, his green eyes twinkling. "I'm sorry I'm late," he said.

Velvet laughed, her fear melting into pure joy. "What took you so long?" she asked.

Laguz got up and came over to her, wrapping his arms around her and holding her to his chest. She breathed in his scent and relaxed into his embrace. "I got held up," he whispered into her hair. "But I'm here now. And I will never leave your side again."

"Promise?" Velvet whispered.

"Promise." Laguz pulled back a little so he could see her face. She stared up at his green eyes.

"I'll love you to infinity," she whispered with a smile, playing with their usual words to match the world they now found themselves in.

He chuckled. "I'll love you to infinity, and beyond."

She laughed in response and reached up to kiss him. Their lips met and stayed connected for several seconds.

Perhaps she could bear to stay for a while to experience this Age of Infinity. With her Flame by her side, and her friends surrounding her, she could do anything.

When they finally broke away from each other, Velvet heard the pitter patter of feet running towards her. She looked down to see a small black dog enthusiastically jumping up. "Oh! Hello! Goodness, you look a lot like-"

"Missy," Laguz said. "Yes, that's what I thought when I saw her. So I had to get her. I don't think she is the Missy we knew, but I remembered you loved the little black dog back in that reality."

Velvet reached out her arms and the little dog jumped into them. Velvet laughed as the dog licked her face. "Does this one have a name?" she asked.

"Well I think Missy suits her, don't you?"

Velvet smiled and stared into her black eyes. "Absolutely." She kissed her on the head and Missy licked her cheek.

"Would you like a cup of tea?" Laguz asked.

Velvet smiled at the normality of his question, after such a hugely magical moment. She nodded and followed him into the kitchen. "So you're on holiday here too?" she asked, realising that she had no idea how he had come to be here.

Laguz shook his head and put the kettle on. "No, I live here. I made a deal with Gold. He wanted me to wait to come to Earth, and he knew that I was desperate to come, to be with you. So I told him he needed to make the wait worth it. So he organised this home for us. He also promised to make all of our dreams come true."

"Our dreams?" Velvet whispered. Her gaze shifted to Laguz's left shoulder and as though she were watching a movie, she saw their lives together in this new age, and she saw them not only growing old together, but growing a family together too. She saw their Earth Angel friends living in a community around them, all living as joyfully and abundantly as was possible. She wondered if this was what Magenta had Seen, and smiled. In all the lives they'd had together, in all the realities and dimensions, she and Laguz had never had children together, never created a family. Until now.

Tears filling her eyes, Velvet whispered. "This is our new home?"

Laguz nodded, seemingly unaware of her having a vision. "It reminds me a little of the cottage in La Rochelle," he said. "And of our home in Atlantis, and in the Seventh. I hope you like it."

Velvet quickly wiped her eyes with her sleeve and shifted Missy in her arms. She smiled at her Flame. "I love it," she said. "I have missed the sea, but most of all, I have missed you."

Laguz stopped making the tea and crossed the room to

where she stood. He wrapped his arms around them both. "Welcome home, my love," he said, leaning down to kiss her again.

Velvet kissed him back, and she knew right then, that there was nowhere else in the universe she would rather be.

Dear Beautiful Reader,

If you have enjoyed this book, and indeed the rest of the Earth Angels Series, please do leave a review online. On whatever platform you purchased it, would be amazing. Every review helps new readers to make the choice whether to give it a try, and reviews on the later books in the series help potential readers to see that the series is worth reading all the way through!

Writing, editing, formatting and publishing these books is very much a labour of love, and other than the help of my amazing friends and family in the editing stage, it is pretty much all up to me to get it done. I don't have a marketing team helping me to spread the word, so if you have enjoyed these books, please do recommend them to your friends, share them on social media or buy them as gifts!

In return for your help, I promise that book 12, the final instalment (I mean it this time) of the series, will be released in a more timely manner than this one was.

Much love and gratitude,

Michelle

xxx

# Gratitude

When I wrote the gratitude for book ten in the Earth Angel Series, I wrote it knowing that it was the end of the series, at least for a long while, and it seems I was right! It has been six years since the release, and so much has shifted and changed in my life, and in the world.

But despite the long pause, my readers have stayed with me, and I have had so much lovely feedback in the last few months, as I have worked on this latest instalment. I want to thank those who have taken the time to reach out and tell me how much they love the series, and how the characters have become their friends, and how much they are looking forward to this one. You have kept me going, kept me focussed on getting it written and published, so thank you, I love you.

Instead of simply repeating the gratitude from book ten, because I still love and appreciate every one of the souls listed there (even if we are no longer in each other's lives); I want to say that the last six years has held some dark times for me and I know for many others, and I am so very thankful for every soul who knowingly or unknowingly helped me through those times. As well as my beautiful mother, my fierce sister and my amazing close friends, there have also been neighbours, strangers and colleagues who have shone their light and encouraged me to keep going.

I am very grateful to my editing/beta team, who have helped me to get this book done on a very short timescale. Thank you to my editor, Liz Lockwood, my continuity expert, Shelley Brookdale, and my betas, Sally Byrne and Lucja Fratczak-Kay. You are all Angels!

As I begin this new chapter in my life, with my little black dog by my side, and my amazing Earth Angel friends and family cheering me on, I couldn't be more grateful for all of the experiences of the last six years that have shaped the person I am now.

# ABOUT THE AUTHOR

Michelle lives in the UK with her little black dog, when she's not flitting in and out of other realms. She is an avid crafter, and enjoys letterpress printing, knitting, sewing, crochet, photography and many other creative pursuits. She has so far written sixteen novels for adults, three for children, a poetry collection and two self-help books.

Please feel free to write a review of this book. Michelle loves to get direct feedback, so if you would like to contact her, please e-mail **theamethystangel@hotmail.co.uk** or keep up to date by following her blog – **TwinFlameBlog.com.** You can also follow her on Instagram **@michellegordonauthor**

To sign up to her mailing list, visit:
# michellegordon.co.uk

# BOOKS BY MICHELLE GORDON

## WHERE'S MY F**KING UNICORN?

Are your bookshelves filled with self-help books, and yet your life feels empty? Do you keep following paths to enlightenment that lead to the same dead ends? You've read the books, attended the seminars and taken heed of every bit of advice going... but you're still waiting for your f**king unicorn to come along! Where's My F**king Unicorn? is a guide to life, creativity and happiness that offers a very different way forward.

Author, Michelle Gordon, explains why, in spite of all your best efforts, your life still doesn't live up to your vision of what it should be, and tells you exactly what you can do about it. In refreshingly down-to-earth language, she shows you how to harness all the self-knowledge you have gained from all those self-help books you've read, and actually start putting it to practical use.

Where's My F**king Unicorn? is published by *Ammonite Press* and is available online and in bookstores.

# THE GIRL WHO LOVED TOO MUCH

What would you do if you suddenly found yourself in a different reality that was better for you, but not for those you loved?

Caru loves to make things. And collect things. And give gifts. She loves to print, sew, knit, paint. Her life is full of unfinished projects, yet devoid of financial stability and romance. Though she loves her life, she finds herself disappointing people and struggling to keep everyone happy.

So when Caru wishes life could be simpler, and then finds herself in a completely different world, where her life is easy, money is abundant, and her long-term boyfriend is the most fabulous cook, she can't quite believe her luck.

But will all her wishes come true? Or will the dream turn into a nightmare?

*The Girl Who Loved Too Much* is a modern day 'It's a Wonderful Life'.

The Girl Who Loved Too Much is published by *Jasper Tree Press* and is available online in eBook and print.

# THE OLD SOUL'S HANDBOOK

It's not easy being an Earth Angel on this planet.
I hope the words within these pages help you in whatever
situation you find yourself in.
Simply ask a question or for guidance, and then open the
book to a random page.
The answers are within.

The Earth Angel Series is published by
*The Amethyst Angel* and is available online in eBook and print.

Not From This Planet is an Independent Publisher on a mission to collaborate with authors to create the best possible books that delight and inspire and entertain – and also pay a fair royalty to the author. They treat every book as if it were their own and they have big have plans to take the publishing world by storm.

Follow Not From This Planet on
Instagram - @notfromthisplanetbooks
Facebook - @notfromthisplanetbooks
Twitter - @ NFTPbooks

NotFromThisPlanet.co.uk